ECHOES OF THE BOAB

J.A. HUNTER

ISBN-13: 978-1-7641203-0-2

Cover design by: Microsoft Co-Pilot
Printed in Australia

For Alex

CONTENTS

PROLOGUE

THE ACCIDENT

The screech of the tires fills the silence of the night's air with a piercing sound. I want to cover my ears, to block it out but my hands and brain aren't working right now.

My eyes frantically dart from one side of the car to the other before locking onto the passenger window to my left. Rain blurs everything; droplets fall fast and alone, but soon they collide, one after another. They rush together like kids pouring out of a crowded assembly hall, all pushing toward the only two small exits.

I snap out of it, shaking my head as if to tell myself to focus on what is really going on because what is really happening is our is car spinning. Endlessly. The rotations feel like they are getting faster and faster, making my stomach lurch into my throat. It's like I am trapped on a wild carnival ride spinning out of control as we hurtle down the remote highway.

I want it to stop!

The noise.

The spinning.

Everything.

But I don't know how, or if it ever will.

I feel useless not being able to control what is happening to me. Even the people I have always relied on to help, to fix things, cannot do a single thing to stop what is happening.

Like a dog burying its bone, her screams are digging a hole deep in my mind, trapping them there with no way for it to escape.

I am confused.

Scared.

Alone.

I am twelve years old.

I am not ready for this.

I want to see my friends.

Tell them I will never be an idiot again.

I want to play football for Australia one day.

I want... my life.

A bleak, grey fog begins to surround our car. It is impossible to tell whether it's the burn from the tires turning to smoke or the dark grey clouds that ignited this deadly storm.

Hard to believe that when I woke this morning there was a blinding stream of light shining through the outer edges of my bedroom window urging me to get up out of bed. Even at lunch, the sky was a stretch of endless blue. After so many dry days, the rain should've felt like relief; cooling everything down that had been overheated for so long.

Instead...

It caused this.

This screeching.

This spinning.

This...

Suddenly I become aware of a pain rising from the tips of my fingers and up my forearms. It's so intense I want to scream; but when I open my mouth, nothing comes out. I look down. My hands are clenched tight; one gripping the door handle, the other yanking the handbrake.

I don't remember pulling it. I just know that when he slammed the brake pedal, yet the car showed no signs of slowing, I panicked. I pulled the handbrake as hard as I could. My fingers still firmly grasping so tightly around it, like they believe it can save us.

"STOP!"

Her screams haunt me, snapping me violently back to the now.

I glance around at the faces beside me. For a moment, they look like strangers. The eyes I share with him. Her dark hair, usually perfect, now tangled and wild.

But it's their expressions that hit the hardest; ones I have never seen before. Pure horror. And as they stare back at me, I know it would be like a mirror, reflecting our shared fear.

Fear.

Shock.

Wonder.

Wondering why this is happening.

Wondering if this is the end.

Wondering if it'll ever stop.

Then I see it. Time seems to freeze.

The smoky grey air that had made it impossible to see only moments ago, suddenly and magically disappears, leaving a clear path to...

What she always talked about.

What she loved.

What she felt connected to.

Even as the car spins, it appears again and again—caught in each 360-degree turn like it's pausing for us, waiting to catch us. Save us.

Unmistakeable with its swollen base for a trunk, leaves beginning to sprout on many of its branches. Looming and towering at the edge of the road. Standing at least 5 metres tall.

Strong. Independent. Resilient.

A boab tree.

Sunlight breaks through the dark grey clouds, shining directly onto the tree making the edges glow as if outlined in gold. We're heading straight for it.

She said we should learn from it.

Protect it.

She said it would...

BANG!

The sound was the loudest, most horrifying noise I have ever heard. The car is pulverised by the huge base of the boab.

The back passenger car door buckle and collapse under the might of it. Fragments shoot through the air, piercing anything in their path.

Him.

Her.

Me.

The car comes to an immediate stop as it folds around the boab, both front and back now facing the same direction.

Everything stops.

Just like I wanted it to.

And it's gone.

The noise.

The spinning.

The pain.

Her.

CHAPTER 1

THE GAME

Today is probably one of the few times the weather couldn't be blamed for my outburst on the football field. I mean, yes it was 35 degrees, but unlike previous wet seasons, the rain had settled in and cooled the air. It had been lashing down for hours; before the game and all through it.

At kick-off, 5pm, the sun had started to lose its fierceness and, more often than not, was hidden by dark menacing clouds threatening to turn violent.

I wish they had. If there'd been a thunderstorm, the

game would have been postponed, and I wouldn't have...

If I am honest, my mood was sour even before the game. In the changerooms earlier, I struggled to put my green strip over my head because I couldn't stop thinking about—couldn't stop *feeling*– the anger from my last chat with Dad.

I mean, why is he always on my case? He knows how to push my buttons. I was just trying to explain my side, but he wouldn't hear it.

It had already been a big week at school, and now I had to share the football field with *them*.

Urgh. I didn't want to be there. I just wanted to put on my JBL headphones, lie on my bed, and let everything wash away. Forgotten.

"Pass me the ball, you idiot!" I snapped.

"I'm trying to," replied Eddie as the black ball crossed over the sideline.

I picked it up and shoved it into Adrian's face. "See this ball? You kick it and it rolls ALL. BY. IT. SELF. Moron!"

"Owen, we're all trying our best," said Colin.

"Well, I guess if you want something done properly, you're better off doing it yourself," I muttered.

Like a snake aggressively seeking out its prey, I ran as

quickly as I could at the opposition player in possession of the ball. I latched onto the ball, my studs connecting like a snake bite, leaving venom shooting through his foot.

I surged forward toward the goal...

Phooweet!

The sound of the whistle infuriated me. I had the ball; I was going to score.

"A YELLOW CARD?! Are you kidding me? You must be blind!" I screamed at the referee.

I pointed at the boy still lying on the ground holding his foot. "He's a wimp, I *barely* touched him. This is a joke!"

Phooweet!

I turn back to face the ref. My mouth dropped open as he held up a second yellow.

Just like that, I was forced to spend the rest of the game watching from the sidelines.

I think to myself that this day couldn't possibly getting any worse.

How wrong I was.

My parents and I walk into the café, the same one we've been coming to since I was born. It looks like it's been here forever.

From what I can remember, the set-up has never changed. It's pretty big, with booths at the back, larger tables with chairs near the front, and a side kitchen where you can see the cook through a small service window. I like watching the waiters collect the food and deliver it to the customers.

The floor is checkered with two different shades of pink but there's also another colour permanently stained on it. The smear of red dirt from outside that is constantly being traipsed through on the bottom of people's shoes without them even noticing. Or caring. Hard not to, though, with the café sitting right off the highway, surrounded by road and red dust.

The staff all know us by name. They even know our orders—though that depends on our mood, which mostly comes down to how the game went... and the car ride over.

"That was a shocking tackle, son," says Dad as we slide into our usual booth.

"Seriously? You think it was worth a yellow card?" I shoot back from across the table.

"Yes! And the second yellow, for your outburst, was definitely warranted. I seriously worry about the man you are becoming, Owen," says Dad, in his best '*I'm disappointed in* *you'*tone.

I pick up the menu like I am reading it, even though I know every item printed on there. I need something to clench, coil behind, to cover my eyes as they turn yellow with venom the longer he talks. I sit upright, rigid, annoyance urging me on.

"Dad, my team is rubbish. I was showing them how to tackle. That ref had no clue. Did you see that other kid tackle Eddie? He didn't get a yellow card!"

Dad leans forward, slumping a bit to meet my eyes. "Owen, that's not the point. What I am trying to tell you, son..."

"Okay, I think we've spent enough time talking about football," cuts in Mum from the seat next to Dad.

Mum's always the peacemaker. She tells Dad when he is being too harsh, which is all the time, and me when I am being a brat, which is most of the time.

We both just smile at her and roll our eyes at each-other when she isn't looking.

It was like that time I got in trouble at school for writing a swear word on my whiteboard during literacy. Dad said the school should have banned me from playing football at the next interschool game instead of the lunch detention they had given me.

I didn't think I deserved any punishment.

Mum said missing lunchtime football with my friends was punishment enough; and told me if I ever wanted to play professionally, I'd still need to pass English.

With her hands pressed under her chin and elbows on the table, Mum smiles and says brightly, "Now, let me guess. For you Owen it'll be the hamburger with wedges. And for Dad the hotdog special?"

Dad gives me a stern look before relaxing his face instantly as he turns gently to Mum. "Honey, I know you don't like it when I am firm with Owen, but he needs to know what he did today was unacceptable."

"Patrick," says Mum as she lovingly puts her hand on his.

We both know what this means. Dad places his other hand over the top of Mum's and bows his head slightly. Once again, she is going to bring peace between us, at least for the moment.

Keeping her hands entwined with Dad's, she turns to me, tilting her head to one side and meeting my gaze with her calm green stare. "Owen, the way you treat others is ultimately how you will be treated. And remembered. We can learn a lot from the Boab Tree..."

Dad and I share a knowing half-smile before droning together, "Muuummm!"

Despite our groans, she smiles. And for the first time, I notice the little wrinkles that form around her eyes. She sees me staring and brushes her forehead like her perfect black hair must be out of place. She tucks it behind her ear, shifts in her seat, then continues.

"It's true. The Boab Tree is a source of life-saving water..."

"Yes, we know, Mum," I interrupt.

"Central wood. Full of moisture. Pulp. Seed pod has Vitamin C," Dad recites like a list of facts he's heard a hundred times before but not really thought about.

He appears to have forgotten that he's mad at me, as he winks in my direction before turning to Mum. "I'm going to regret asking, but I will... what do Boab Trees and Vitamin C have to do with Owen's behaviour and how you treat people?"

"Well... I'm glad you asked," Mum says, grinning, her eyes playfully bouncing between Dad and me.

"Here we go," I laugh, resting both elbows on the table in front of me and pretending to hide behind my open hands.

Mum crosses her arms, slumps back in her seat and then begins in a confident manner. "The Boab survives in the hottest of climates, yet, the pulp from the seed pod produces high levels of Vitamin C. So, no matter what external factors impact upon you, you must be of strong character and help others in any way that you can."

"A bit of a stretch honey," says Dad while playfully miming with his hands an invisible elastic band being pulled in and out.

Shaking my head, I throw my hands up. "I don't get it. But I *do* get 'shot-gun' on the way home."

"That's not how it works Owen and you know it," smirks Mum as she raises from her slumped position. "If you want the front seat, you have to play for it," she declares.

"Aren't I getting too old for playing these kid games?" I ask, pretending they annoy me.

"You'll always be my kid," she says. "And besides, you *want* to sit in the front seat, don't you?"

I sigh, pretending to be bored. "Yeah."

Mum nods to herself. "Well, I'm going to make you earn it for as long as I can get away with it."

"Okay, let's play then," I say still acting like I don't care.

CHAPTER 2
DOCTOR SIMMONS

I hear talking.

What are they saying? I can't quite make out the words.

Are they talking about me?

Do they know I am lying here, listening?

One voice is so familiar. It's a man. He's not saying much; I can just hear fragments of murmuring when the other man takes a breath. The tone is so familiar. The way he... I think... it's my dad.

Who is Dad speaking to?

I scrunch up my face and tilt my head, hoping to block out the constant humming noise which is causing this unbelievable throbbing inside my skull.

Oh- ouch!

I become aware of increasingly sharp pains stabbing through different parts of my body.

Why do my cheekbones hurt?

My neck?

Oww, my shoulder. My...

"Yes... my assessment... blunt trauma," he says.

As the words become clearer, my thoughts of pain are pushed aside.

Blunt trauma?

What does that mean?

Someone tell me something; I don't understand what you are saying.

"We believe our surgical team got..."

Surgical team?

My dad's speaking to...

A doctor? A team of doctors?

Surgical? Did I have surgery?

Please, someone has to tell me what's going on. I *think* I'm saying this all aloud; for someone to hear me, to realise

I'm lying right here, that I'm alive.

But it's all just a conversation in my head.

"Yes, timing is everything with eye traumas, but we'll know more once he wakes and we begin rehab," says who I now think is a doctor.

"Okay, but will... my son ever be able to see again?" asks Dad.

See again?

Eye trauma?

I *can* see; what is he talking about?

I'm just resting.

My eyes are closed because I'm too tired and too sore to do anything else.

If I really wanted to, I could open them.

I pause.

The thought of not seeing again shocks me into denial.

He can't be talking about *me*.

Maybe that voice isn't even my dad's. Maybe the reason the talking is so muffled is because it's coming from a different room.

It's not me. It can't be.

I can see.

My thoughts are interrupted by the sound of the doctor

clearing his throat.

"In most cases, full sight is restored within the first six months."

"In most cases? And what about the other cases?" Dad's voice is filled with panic.

The doctor replies instantly and in a matter-of-fact way. "It's very rare. And like I said we treated the trauma in a very timely manner; within 4hrs of impact. Considering where you were, travel time... I'd say that leaves us in a very good position."

"Yes, but ...?" interrupts Dad.

"In rare cases, he may continue to be sensitive to light, see only outlines or have blurred vision. Or, in the most severe, rare case, Owen may never regain his sight," says the doctor.

The air falls silent.

The humming suddenly stops, as if someone has flicked a switch.

I've been trying to convince myself that it wasn't me; even though... I remember.

I remember *everything*.

The impact.

The deafening sound it made.

The shards of glass flying through the air.

My head smashing against the upper part of the passenger door.

Her.

I can't stand this anymore.

He said it. I heard him.

He said my name.

The only way to know for sure is to open my eyes.

He said I might never regain my sight.

Just do it! I *have* to know.

Okay, on the count of three.

Here I go.

Do it.

1... 2... 3...

I open my eyes; and at the same time, I hear a voice: "Owen?"

But I ignore the voice.

Because it's dark.

Completely, pitch black.

There's nothing.

No!

It's not true. I must be dreaming.

I need to wake up from this nightmare, or someone

needs to turn on the lights.

"Owen?"

The voice calls again.

Hot flushes rise from my neck and fill my cheeks.

My stomach clenches like acid is rising through it, a toxic ache climbing from the pit of my stomach to my chest and settling in my throat.

I feel like I'm going to throw up.

But before I can, the voice interrupts my thoughts again; and this time, I pay attention.

It's the doctor.

"Can you hear me? Owen, my name is Doctor Simmons. If you can hear me, is it okay if I put my hand in yours so you can give it a squeeze?"

Pause.

"Good job mate, that's a tight squeeze for a 10-year-old," he says as if trying to lighten the mood.

But it only irritates me.

I squirm on the bed, trying to make myself appear bigger than I must seem right now, and say through a raspy voice, "I'm twelve."

Through a stifled laugh, the doctor responds more seriously, "Oh, well that makes much more sense, Owen.

Now, I know you can't see me right now because of those patches we've got covering your eyes, but I am your doctor. I'm looking after you. My name is—"

"Patches?" I ask hastily.

"Yes, they need to stay on for the next few days, you've been through..."

His voice trails off.

I feel relief.

I *thought* I was blind.

My body relaxes.

Shoulders fall.

Back arches as I slump down.

Legs lay flat.

The sick feeling I had begins to ease, the acid sliding back down the path it came from.

I'm feeling sleepy again. And even though thoughts try to creep in, while pain shoots off like fireworks in my head, my tiredness overwhelms me, and I fall into a deep sleep.

* * *

The most excruciating pain I've ever felt in my entire twelve years wakes me from the deepest sleep. I scream in absolute agony as what sounds like a herd of people rush toward me. They give brief, direct instructions to each other all the while speaking to me in warm, calming tones.

"Hi Owen, my name is Lucy. I am a nurse, are you in pain?" she asks while placing her hand on my shoulder.

I nod feverishly.

Then I hear her again, "Don't worry; we'll take care of that discomfort for you, honey. I am going to give you something for the pain. It'll make you feel better, but also might make you quite sleepy, okay?"

"Nothing to worry about sweetie," comes a second voice from the other side of the bed as another hand strokes my head.

I take a deep breath.

The scurry of footsteps slows.

The voices stop.

It's then I realise; the pain is beginning to ease.

And with that, I am taken again by the tiredness.

Once more, I fall into a deep sleep.

CHAPTER 3

I-SPY A NEW BEGINNING

We've been driving for ages. I look out the window, pretending I can see all the same boring things I always have; the lined red dirt road, the occasional tree whooshing past, and the endless horizon. Who'd want to be able to see that anyway?

When I was younger, we went on long family road trips, just the three of us. Mum and I would play I-Spy in between sleeping and eating her famous chicken sandwiches. We started off with easy things to spy like 'road' and 'tree'. Then, as I got older and the game became too easy, Mum got really creative; well, that's what she called it. I called it impossible.

The game turned into a mix of I-Spy and charades. She would mime, putting up fingers to show how many words, then sway side to side with both hands out, as if to say it was something we could see.

I remember the last time I played. I just gave up. I couldn't guess what it was, even with all of her so-called brilliant clues. Turns out it was, *slow-moving tractor.* Mum tried to explain the hyphenated word by drawing an invisible line in the air with her finger. She did it slower and slower, like that would help. I didn't even know what a hyphen was. I've never been good at that English stuff; or any school stuff, really.

"How much longer until we're there?" I ask Dad impatiently.

"We're 'bout 20 minutes out," he replies, his tone suggesting he's lost in his own thoughts.

How is this town going to be any different from our old one? I want to be back at our house; the one I know so well. I know where everything is.

I've been there since I was born. It's the only home I've ever known. I know where all the furniture is. All the doors—those that stay closed and those that are always open.

The exact path from the front door to my bedroom. It isn't fair.

Mum and Dad moved into that house right after they got married. It was a wedding gift from my Mum's parents: my grandma and grandpop.

I could tell you about the chip in my bedroom doorframe from when I had the biggest tantrum as a little kid.

Or about the stain on the lounge room floor. Mum was so mad at herself when she spilled juice there.

Dad and I teased her for months afterward because, just five days after getting the carpets professionally cleaned, she knocked over her glass of juice resting on the lounge. It made a giant puddle. No cleaning product could fix it. Eventually, she bought a side table to cover it— though it meant you'd bang your knee if you weren't careful walking into the room.

"Here we are, Owen. We've reached the town of Wanooni. See?" says Dad.

"Oh yeah, Dad, I can *see* everything perfectly," I snap.

"I... I... it's just a figure of speech. I wasn't thinking," he says, apologetically.

I sigh and rest my chin on my hand, my elbow leaning

against the door. I know Dad didn't mean it, but I'm just so... I don't know. Everything's just... I don't know.

My forehead presses against the cool passenger window; it's a relief in this heat. I feel the car slow. I can make out small buildings, people, and trees by their outlines.

Trees?

Wait- is that a ...?

I recognise it, even with my poor vision.

It's a boab.

In the middle of town?

I must have let out a gasp or something, because Dad, as if reading my thoughts, mutters, "Wow, a boab tree in the town centre, right next to the corner store."

Such a strange place for a boab, I think, feeling a sudden rush of anger which takes me by surprise.

"Do you want to sss... do you want me to drive past your school?" Dad asks hesitantly.

I don't answer. If I do, it'll be the anger that spills out.

"I know we won't be able to go in," he says. "Just thought we could start getting our bearings of the town."

"Nah. I'm tired, I just want to get to the house and sleep," I say sharply.

"That's okay. I'm a bit tired too," he replies quickly,

trying to ease the tension. "Plenty of time to get to know the town. No need to rush— otherwise there won't be much to do after that," he chuckles.

I shake my head and continue looking out the window, trying to process shapes and outlines that used to be so clear. I squint, trying to focus— but even at this slow speed, things rush past too quickly to figure them out.

The *sounds* though— those are crystal clear. I don't know how to explain it, but I can hear so much better than before. I can hear Dad breathing like his mouth is centimetres from my ear. Even his subtle movements, like his clothing brushing up against itself; similar to the sound of rustling leaves on a windy, autumn day. Maybe it was the bang. Maybe the accident did something. The doctor said I'd rely more on other senses like hearing and touch. I guess this is what he meant.

The car slows almost to a stop. I feel the rough surface beneath the tires vibrating through me. We turn.

The vibrations quicken, then stop. I hear the keys clank and the engine sputter out.

We're here.

There's a dark rectangular shape in front of me— about the size of a house with three bedrooms and two bathrooms.

The sun must be setting behind it because the outline glows at the edges.

The brightness of the drive made me wear sunglasses. The doctor told me to wear them outdoors to protect my eyes. Since the accident, I've been super sensitive to light. I hate the sunglasses. I can only imagine how stupid I look in them.

"Okay, here we are. I can get the bags later. Let's go check it out," says Dad getting out of the car.

We bought a second-hand car last week; a green Volvo sedan. Dad says it's one of the safest cars on the market.

I don't think any car is safe anymore.

Before I can go too far down that thought, I'm startled by the sound of my car door opening. I automatically grab my seatbelt, lean back, hold my breath. My body braces as if for impact. I clench the belt tight.

"Owen?" Dad says, concern in his voice.

I snap out of it, release the belt, and shake my body to loosen up. But I'm still mad.

"What!?" I yell.

He pauses.

"Hold onto my arm. It's next to your left. I'll help you get to the front door."

I sigh loudly, then feel for his arm and grab it. He guides me across what feels like a gravel driveway, then grass. No uneven surfaces so far.

Then I feel his hands on my shoulders, gently pulling me back.

"We'll get stair strips to help you manage these better. Lina from the hospital said..."

"There shouldn't be stairs! Why would you pick a house with stairs?" I shout.

"Most houses here have stairs. This was the only..."

"Great. I'm trapped," I mutter, pulling away from him and stubbornly taking the stairs on my own.

I feel for the railing with my right hand before grasping it. Then I begin to raise my left foot trying to get a feel for the height of the first step before placing my full weight on it. Once my left foot is up, the right foot simply follows to sit next to it. I slide my hand further up the railing and then the next few steps are a case of repeating the first. It gets easier— becomes instinctual. I got a lot of practice in rehab.

We walk down what Dad says is a wooden-floored entryway. I hear him jingling keys.

"That's the one," he says, unlocking the door with a click, followed by a long squeak as it opens.

A wave of musty, trapped air hits me. It smells stale and sharp— like something old and shut up for too long.

I feel Dad place my hands on his shoulders.

"Hold on. I'll lead. Mind the door lip," he says.

I step over the entry with an exaggerated stride and follow him, hands on his shoulders. It's awkward, but it's the best option in an unfamiliar place.

We walk down a narrow hallway. I can almost *feel* the walls close in on me. Claustrophobic.

Suddenly, light. I squint as a stream dazzles me. Must be a big room.

"This is the kitchen, dining, and TV room. Nice open-plan living," says Dad, imitating the real estate agent.

I roll my eyes.

We turn, and I brush against a doorway. A few more steps.

"This'll be your room. I'm giving you the master— comes with an ensuite. Should make life easier," Dad says like he's done me a huge favour.

As if this makes up for everything.

For what he did.

For how he ruined everything.

But for that, I can never forgive.

I realise now's not the time to start another argument so I manage a thanks before telling him I am tired and reach out for the rectangular shape I can see under the window. The soft, silky familiar feeling tells me I was right, it is my bed.

At least some things have stayed the same I think to myself. I turn, stretch my hands down until I feel the doona and then sit down. I can make out Dad's silhouette still standing in the middle of the room.

"Want me to bring in some dinner later? Help you have a shower or unpack your suitcase?" he asks.

"No! I told you, I'm tired," I snap.

"Well, okay. I guess I'll talk to you tomorrow then," he says, voice soft and wounded.

I put on my headphones, blocking out everything and everyone.

I want everything to stop. Especially my thoughts.

But I know I can never stop thinking about...

The anger bubbles up inside of me like a volcano ready to erupt. I can't believe he has made us move to this house. To this town. It's like he thinks we will just forget about everything.

Forget. Just because we're not there.

Because she's not here.

But I can never forget.

And I won't ever.

CHAPTER 4

LINA & THE FALSE START

The light screams in through the window, illuminating my bedroom like a car's headlights shining into your eyes on full beam. It's the vertical blinds. They are so old, many don't even close properly. They're fixed at an angle that lets the light seep in.

My bed is positioned directly under the window— a poor choice by the movers yesterday, but one I was too tired to notice, let alone correct last night.

The light hurts my eyes unless I am wearing my sunglasses. It's like staring directly into the sun. I squint, my eyes water, and a dull ache begins to fill my head. The doctor says if my recovery goes to plan, this sensitivity will eventually stop; but right now, in the early hours of the morning, it hasn't. If I don't wear my sunglasses or manage to block out the light, it feels like my head might explode behind my eyeballs.

I remember one time, shortly after I left the hospital, I spent a bit of time in the backyard without my sunglasses. Before long, I was in agony. The pain wasn't like a normal headache; it was blinding, throbbing and completely excruciating.

We went back to the hospital that day, and Dr. Simmons explained that while my eyes are recovering, even the slightest bit of light puts extreme strain on them. They have to work extra hard to adjust, which causes migraine-like headaches.

I press the button on my watch and the robotic voice drones out the time. It's 5:13am. I put on my sunglasses and reach for my headphones. They're still strung around the top of my bed where I left them last night before I fell asleep. I hit play, close my eyes, and wait for the pain in my head to subside. I like wearing my headphones, they block out the noise and help me relax.

Moments later, I jolt upright at the sensation of a hand resting on my shoulder. I take off my headphones, open my eyes and immediately see a figure standing over my bed. "Everything, okay?"

My eyes adjust slightly, but it's the voice I recognise first. It's Dad.

The question irritates me, and with my head still pounding, I lash out. "Are you serious? How can everything be okay?"

"I just heard a noise coming from your room and wanted to check you were alright," he says gently.

Under my sunglasses, I shoot a glare in his direction, imagining I'm burning holes through his eyes that escape out the back of his head.

When I don't respond, he tries again. "You're wearing your sunglasses."

"Yeah, I kinda had to, didn't I?" I snap, gesturing toward the window where the light is pouring in.

He doesn't say anything.

"The light," I add sharply.

More silence.

"It's coming through the blinds and giving me a headache."

"This'll all be fixed, Owen. The lady said she'll prepare the house to make it more comfortable for you. Block-out blinds. Light strips on the floors and on the steps out front," he replies.

"Whatever," I mutter, putting my headphones back on to signal that this conversation is over. It works. He stands there for a moment, motionless, before his silhouette moves away and I hear the door close.

I wake again hours later to soft voices outside my door. I tune in, using my supersonic hearing, trying to understand the whispers and figure out who's speaking. At least losing my vision has some advantages. Sometimes.

"Yes, I will have a chat to Owen," says a woman whose voice sounds familiar.

Then comes Dad. I recognise his voice immediately. "I think it will help him to adjust, if it comes from someone else. I just don't know what to do anymore. Everything I say, he explodes. He's so angry all the time. He was difficult before the accident, but now... it's worse. She always knew what to say. How to deal with him. I can't do it without her. I don't know. I'm sorry... Anyway, how about a cuppa?"

On the wooden floors I can easily make out the sound

of their footsteps fading away as they walk further from my room. Their voices fade until I can't hear them anymore.

I know she won't leave until she's spoken to me. I know who she is— Lina. I met her on my last day at the hospital. She seems nice, but we don't need her help. I don't want it. I'll be seeing again in no time, and she'll just start pushing for school like she did in the hospital.

I'm not ready for that. I just need more time. What am I going to learn, anyway? I can't read or write like this. I can't play sport. It's pointless.

I carefully make my way to the door, following the sound of the kettle boiling to the kitchen, hoping there's nothing in my path that'll trip me up in the narrow hallway.

I stand at the doorway, waiting for one of them to see me. I bet with myself who will rush over first.

"Owen? You should've called out. I would have come to get you."

Sure enough, it's Dad. He helps me through what he says are packing boxes and unfamiliar furniture, guiding me to the couch. I see the outline of another person sitting. She stands.

"Good morning, Owen. Do you remember me?"

"Yes. You're Lina," I reply, hesitant despite being 100%

certain.

"That's right. You've got a good memory for voices. How's your vision? Any improvement?" she asks, getting straight to the point. I like that about her.

"The same," I reply.

"That's to be expected. You have already made such great progress. If you remain patient and keep up the exercises, I am sure you will make further gains in no time," concludes Lina.

I hate the exercises.

My mind drifts back to the hospital; the first time they took the eye patches off. I prayed every day for that whole week that I'd wake up and see again. I'd never prayed before, didn't believe in that kind of stuff, but I was ready to believe if it meant I'd open my eyes and have perfect vision again.

Dr. Simmons kept warning me not to get my hopes up. He said that even if I couldn't see yet, it didn't mean I never would. But I didn't want *maybe*. I wanted to play football again.

Lina's voice pulls me back to the present.

"Now, how about school, Owen?"

There it is. The topic I knew was coming. I can feel

Dad lean in, like he's holding his breath. Or maybe it's just my imagination.

"I'm not ready yet," I say sharp and certain.

"I know you don't want to hear this, but school will help you— both with recovery and academically. You've already missed two months, and it would've been more if not for the timing of the holidays. We were lucky," says Lina.

"Lucky? In what universe was I lucky?" I shout.

"That's not what I meant, Owen, and you know it. Your dad moved you here so that you can receive a top education; one that supports students learning braille and provides quality one-on-one support. You can't focus only on the negatives, when there are plenty of positives."

That's Lina for you, always taking Dad's side. Always cutting through my nonsense. She tells you what you need to do, how to do it, and why. I remember her saying she has seven kids of her own. No wonder she's like this; efficient and to the point.

"I'm not ready for school," I repeat, standing up this time to show I will not be backing down on this.

"This is no longer a negotiation, Owen. You've been enrolled. You start at Wanooni District tomorrow. It might not be what you want, but it's what you need. You'll see. I'll check in again in a few days."

She stands and leaves abruptly. That's her way of having the last word.

I hear the front door open and close. I'm frozen. I can't believe how the conversation ended.

Dad hasn't moved from the couch. My mouth hangs open; words stuck in my throat. I want to ask him why he didn't speak up. Why he didn't take my side? But he never has. So why would he start now?

I want to yell. I want to scream at Lina that I don't have to go; that I don't want to go. But she's already gone.

Instead, I close my mouth. Then I start walking, slowly, following the scent of Lina's perfume. I make my way through the kitchen entrance, then the narrow hallway, hands gliding along the walls. It's hard in the dim light, but after what feels like the right number of steps, I reach out for the front door.

At first, I can't find the handle. I step forward, try again. Still nothing. One more step— and there it is. I find it, turn the knob, and ease the door open.

I am relieved to feel a slight breeze on my face and light flood my vision.

"Owen, what are you doing?" Dad yells from behind.

"I am going for a walk, don't follow me," I shout back.

I pause, waiting to hear him stop me. To say it's too dangerous. To say I don't have to go to school until I'm ready.

But he says nothing.

So, I slide on my sunglasses, step over the lip, and close the door behind me. Panic and exhilaration wash over me as I head out— alone— for the first time in months.

CHAPTER 5

THE MEETING PLACE

I take my time walking down the stairs of our new house, despite the urge to sprint down them as fast as I can, creating distance between myself and this life I never wanted. In our old town, I was allowed to ride my bike, walk to the shops, and hang out with friends, as long as I messaged Mum to say where I'd be and when I'd be home. But since the accident, Dad hasn't let me do any of that. I feel trapped, claustrophobic; especially with him working from home and barely leaving the house. It's like I have become a baby again. Everyone thinks I can't look after myself.

I stride out more confidently once I feel the soft grass underfoot, remembering how flat it had felt yesterday. Not far ahead, I see a large shape moving quickly across my field of vision. Judging by its size and the gentle hum of an engine, I decide it's a car and realise I'm nearing the street. I slow my pace, not wanting to attract attention; but quickly realise the shape is shrinking, and the sound is fading. I shake my head. No one around here knows me. It's normal for a twelve-year-old boy to walk along the street he lives on.

Suddenly, I feel gravel crunch under my shoes. I've made it to the end of the driveway and the edge of the road. I smile at this small achievement, then let out a laugh— half proud, half embarrassed. This whole situation is ridiculous.

The street is quiet, as you'd expect on a weekday morning in a small town. I take a deep breath, look both ways out of instinct, listen closely, then step out onto the road. The surface is smooth beneath my feet. I walk cautiously, one foot in front of the other, straining my eyes and bending down to get the most out of what little vision I have through my sunglasses. To anyone watching, I probably look like I've dropped something or like Wanooni's very own hunchback.

I feel loose gravel underfoot again— I've made it to the other side. I decide the safest thing is to walk along the edge of the street with one foot on the smooth road and the other on the gravel, letting the texture guide me.

I keep walking, listening carefully for cars. My body starts to relax. I walk more upright now, still watching my steps.

Then, suddenly, both feet are on smooth surface. I stop immediately.

What's going on?

I turn my head in every direction, pivoting on the spot. My pulse quickens. I try to steady my thoughts. Don't panic. Not now. Not when I'm out alone for the first time in months, in a place where I know no one, and I can barely see.

I notice my breathing. It's short, rapid.

I need to calm down.

I start counting out loud, pressing my fingers one by one to my thumb.

One. Index on thumb.

Two. Middle finger.

Three. Ring finger.

Four. Little finger.

Five. Back to index.

By the time I reach twenty, I'm calm again. It's the only thing that works when I am really scared or angry. After the accident, Dr. Simmons and Dad made me see the hospital psychologist. He taught me this strategy. It's probably the one thing that actually works; stopping my thoughts from going into a loop.

I feel anger and hurt bubble up again, so I push those thoughts aside and focus on my surroundings.

I squint to my left, trying to make sense of the blurry outlines. They seem familiar— but I can't quite place them.

Then I remember. When we arrived yesterday and drove through town to our house, there was...

The building.

The tree.

Next to each other.

Just as Dad described them.

It's the corner store, right beside the big boab tree in the middle of town.

I face it fully now, one foot in the gravel, the other on the smooth road.

Something draws me toward it. My legs start moving on their own, like there's a magnetic force pulling me in.

As I approach, I tune into the town's sounds. People chatting, a baby crying, a car humming by, a door slamming, a dog barking.

But I block it all out.

By the time I'm standing next to the boab, it's quiet in my head again. I place my hand on the wide trunk and trail my fingers along its surface as I slowly walk around it. It must be two, maybe three metres around, and three or four metres high.

I smile to myself, remembering how Mum loved the short, stout ones the best. She said they symbolised physical and mental toughness. I'm not sure how she came up with that. I just think the tall ones could be mistaken for other trees— but not this one. This one is unmistakably a boab.

It's still the wet season, but this tree's leaves are sparse— probably because of where it's planted. I wouldn't like living here either.

At least you're living, I think bitterly.

Anger and sadness rise inside me. My eyes begin to burn—not from trauma, but from the tears I'm trying to hold back. I grit my teeth, hoping that will stop them. It doesn't. So, I kick the trunk of the boab. Just quick jabs at first, then harder, even though it's hurting me more than the tree.

I'm about to punch it when a calm, gentle voice interrupts me.

"It's a thing of true beauty," says a woman who I am not sure is speaking to me. I keep still, facing the tree, hoping she'll leave.

"They're majestic wouldn't you say? The twisted branches, bulbous trunk, green leaves... all combining into something mysterious. You really have to see them to believe it," she continues.

Her voice is soft, her tone light, but there's something powerful in it. She's clearly not taking the hint. Without turning around, I say, as politely as I can manage, "I'd like to be alone."

She ignores me. "They're not just beautiful, you know. They're useful too."

This time I turn around to face her so she can see that I am not in the mood for this nonsense, but as I do, I am intrigued by the small, slim shadow in front of me. Obviously, I can't make out any facial features although I imagine she's smiling right now. I can't explain it. It's a feeling and this feeling tones down what I say to her next.

"Look, it's cool you seem to know so much, but I don't care about boab trees. I have asked you nicely to leave me alone, please just leave me alone," I say.

Again, she doesn't move. She also doesn't speak. Maybe she's finally gotten the message.

I turn back to the tree. But I can feel her eyes on me, and it makes me feel... weird. I don't quite understand it. But anger quickly pushes that aside.

Anger at everything—

At my life.

At Dad.

At this town.

At this woman.

I turn around again.

"Are you deaf? I said go away!" I shout.

She still just stands there, wearing this ridiculously big, floppy hat; or at least, that's what I assume it is.

Then I notice a throbbing in my toe. A wet feeling spreads through the front of my shoe.

She rushes forward, reading my mind. Startled, I feel her shoulder under my arm as she supports me.

"You're bleeding," she says. "Tell me which way is home. I'll make sure you get there, okay?"

I can't believe how kind she's being after how I treated her. It's like she understands my anger isn't really aimed at her. Like she's listening. Like she cares.

She wants to help.

It's not long before we reach my driveway, then the stairs. She gently places my hand on the railing. I take the steps slowly, hobbling. At the top, a shape I instantly recognise is waiting.

It's Dad.

His voice is shaky. He asks where I've been and what happened to my foot. He's worried. I don't think he wanted me to leave the house earlier; but he knew he had to let me.

"I'm fine, Dad. I just need a shower and a rest."

I glance behind me, wondering why he hasn't said anything to the woman; but she's gone.

"What is it, Owen? What are you looking for?" Dad asks.

"No," I say quickly, even though it doesn't answer his question. I'm just relieved she didn't stick around to explain what happened at the boab.

Then, out of nowhere, a thought enters my head:

I hope I see her again.

I give Dad a weak smile. It surprises me. I think it surprises him too.

And then I head inside.

CHAPTER 6

A SENSE OF DEJA VU

"How was your shower?" Dad asks as we make our way into the lounge room.

"Fine," I reply.

"That foot looks a bit nasty. Let me get the medical kit and take a look at it," he says, mind made up.

I shrug my shoulders as he helps me onto the couch, and I let myself sink into it.

"Now, where did I put that medical kit?" Dad mutters rhetorically; he is the only one who packed all of the boxes, so he's the only one who could know.

"Here it is. I've got it," he announces a moment later.

He walks back into the room, now clear of packing boxes. The layout is simple: one three-seater couch, a side table, and a flat-screen television mounted on the wall. I know this because Dad told me about fifty times in the car on the way here. He was adamant that, until I fully regain my sight, we don't need anything that might trip me up. Dad's always been practical like that.

He sits down beside me, then lifts my leg gently onto his thigh.

"Looks like you did a good job," he says.

I don't respond; just grimace as he taps and grips around my foot. Everything from my toes to my heel throbs. Dad tells me there's a lot of bruising and that my big toenail has come off completely. He cleans the wound and wraps it in a small bandage. The whole process gives me an eerie sense of déjà vu. To my surprise, Dad says nothing; not once asking how I hurt it or assuming I'd gotten myself into trouble.

When he's done, he places two tablets in my hand and gives me a glass of water.

"It'll help with the pain."

"Do you remember that time you hurt your ankle at

soccer? Sorry; football," he corrects himself quickly.

"Yeah," I reply hesitantly, unsure where this is going.

"It blew up like a balloon, didn't it? You were in so much pain; thought it was broken. But it turned out to be a really bad sprain."

With my leg still resting on his thigh, he gently squeezes my ankle.

"You were on crutches for a week. Had all those exercises to do. Then when you were finally back playing again, I'd strap your ankle. Remember?"

"I remember," I say, a slight smile forming. That was the best year of football; and not just because we made the finals.

We sit in silence; both lost in our own memories. Even though I'd been injured, I remember that time fondly. It was one of the few times I felt like Dad really paid attention to me.

He was so invested in my recovery. He'd make time every evening to do the exercises with me. We used to joke that *he* was the one with the sprained ankle because he had such a hard time balancing.

Every morning he'd ask how the swelling was and check in about my pain level before a game.

But the next season, once I didn't need the ankle strapping anymore, he stopped asking. Stopped coming to most of my games. Work got in the way. And even when he did show up, he was usually on the phone or sending emails, not even facing the field.

Mum would nudge him if it looked like we were going to score. Sometimes he'd catch the moment. Sometimes he'd miss it.

I remember asking him about a play earlier this season; it was a perfect passing sequence. His response made it clear he hadn't been watching. When I pushed him about it, he got defensive and brought up the time I missed an open goal. That turned into a big argument. After that, I stopped asking him what he thought. Stopped caring if he was even there.

Mum would try to smooth things over, dropping easy questions into the conversation; stuff like, *'Wasn't that a great pass to Eddie who scored?'* So Dad could just nod and agree, pretending he'd seen it too.

My brief moment of warm, happy memories cools before turning to ice. The more I think about, the more annoyed I get. The tension builds inside me until something I notice snaps me out of it.

A shape. A distinct outline. One I could never forget.

It's the photo frame. Hexagonal. I can't see the photo clearly, but I don't need to. I know exactly what's inside. It's the wedding photo of Mum and Dad, standing in front of the boab tree at Knight's Park, taken not long after they moved it from Warmun.

Dad must notice me staring because he gently lowers my leg and stands up. He walks over to the photo, picks it up, then returns to the couch.

"This is the wedding photo of me and your mum. Knight's Park, late 2008," he says.

"I know," I mutter.

"Your mum couldn't believe our luck. The year we got married, they moved a thirty-tonne boab to the big smoke. She loved those trees growing up in the Gagossa, they were everywhere. She missed them when she moved to the city for work."

There's a sadness in his voice. Thick. Like air trapped in a balloon, swelling with pressure.

And I feel that pressure too. I want to escape it.

The sadness.

The anger.

All of it.

"It's so stupid!" I snap, yelling at him. "They're just trees. So what if her parents planted a boab seed the day she was born? No one cares! It didn't help her. It did the opposite. It's done!"

I cannot bear to be in the same room as him anymore. The lounge room which is open and spacious feels as though it is caving in around me. I get up, carefully at first, then move quicker down the hallway, arms outstretched, brushing both walls so I don't lose balance.

At the door to my room, I turn.

"You should hate it just as much as me," I shout, then slam the door.

I lean against it, my shoulders rising and falling. I'm exhausted. Tired of who I am. Tired of fighting. I fumble my way to my bed.

I need to rest.

I need my headphones.

I need to stop these thoughts inside my head.

I need...

One. Index finger to thumb.

Two. Middle finger.

Three ...

I lay down on my bed, now moved away from the

window. Dad must have shifted it after he helped me with the shower this morning.

A pang of guilt hits me. My mouth goes dry. He's trying. I know he is.

I stay on top of the sheets, too hot and restless to get under them. My body is a perfect reflection of my mind; both agitated and overwhelmed. I reach for my headphones and turn them on.

The familiar sounds of guitar, then drums. Instrumental versions of my favourite pop songs. Familiar. I let the music take me. Let it carry me away.

And eventually, I drift off with the music still thrumming through my headphones.

CHAPTER 7
THE NIGHTMARE

"Today's the day, Owen. Are you excited?" Dad asks.

I really was; finally, they were going to remove the eye patches I have been wearing since the surgery. But for some reason, my excitement is tangled up with anxiety. All these negative thoughts crash through my mind like waves pounding the shore.

And what comes out of my mouth isn't ideal:

"Let's just get this over with," I say.

"Hello!" says Dr. Simmons cheerily as I hear his

footsteps draw closer to the bed where I'm sitting upright.

"It's D-Day, my O-man. Ha! O-man... o-men. I'd say that's a good omen, wouldn't you?" He lets out the loud, distinctive laugh I've come to know all too well over the last few...

Days?

Weeks?

I'm not even sure how long it's been.

I hear Dad laugh along, probably encouraging him. I stay silent, which doesn't go unnoticed by Dr. Simmons.

"One day you'll laugh at my jokes, Owen. They're good; I surprise even myself," he says.

"Sure," I reply, trying to sound even, although I know my voice comes out shaky. I can't relax. Not when I'm about to find out whether I'll ever see again.

"Alright, enough about me. Let's take those patches off. Now remember, Owen; don't expect everything to be high definition, like you kids seem to expect these days."

He slips out of his clown voice and seamlessly into his serious-surgeon one.

"Your eyes need time to adjust. And remember what I've said; if you can't see properly today, it doesn't mean you never will. It might just take more time. Also, the light will be overwhelming, so I recommend opening your eyes slowly.

Blink a few times. Let them adjust."

He seems to easily flip between the clown comedian and the serious surgeon.

"Okay," I say, absorbing every word like they're instructions for survival. For the first time in my life, I wonder if there's a wrong way to open your eyes. I smile at this silly thought.

"I am going to take off one patch at a time, Owen. Let's start with your left eye," he says, like a game-show host revealing what's the mystery prize behind door number one.

I feel the patch pulling at my skin. The sticky adhesive clings desperately to my cheek like sap on a tree. Eventually, it lets go. Even with my eye still shut, light pours in. My eyeball twitches beneath the lid, struggling to adjust to the change.

In that moment, I wonder if I want to open them at all. What is there that I want to see anyway?
Is it even worth it?

Dr. Simmons interrupts my spiral:

"The nurse is going to wipe your eye with a warm cloth. Then we'll let you know when you can open it."

A gentle warmth touches my eyelid; soft, slow wipes from the inner corner to the outer edge. Then... nothing.

Silence.

For a moment, panic creeps in. What if something's wrong? What if they're about to tape the patch back on and say there's nothing they can do?

Dr. Simmons's booming voice cuts through. "Take your time. When you're ready, you can open your eye."

The room feels like a tunnel. All the sounds around me echo. My breathing is loud. I hear a monitor beeping outside the room. It's overwhelming.

Maybe I'm not ready.

Maybe they'll get called away and I won't have to do this. Maybe I shouldn't.

But then...

What if I *can* see?

That thought.

That hope.

That moment.

It silences everything. My breathing slows. The background noise fades. It's just me now. And it's now or never.

I slowly begin to open my eye.

The instant I do, an unbearable snap of light that feels

like a slap to my face blasts me. Reflexively, I slam it shut again. Squeezing it tight.

"That's it, Owen. Whenever you're ready. Each time will get easier," says Dr. Simmons, calm and steady.

It's like he's reading my mind, but I wonder if he realises just how powerful the light is. I trust him, even though his jokes are really bad. He's been a good doctor; explained everything simply so that I can understand, but at the same time not treated me like a child. Sometimes he steps in when Dad and I argue.

The thought distracts me for a while but I know it's time. I can't delay any longer. I steel myself. Then try again.

The light punches in again, but I keep the eye open this time. My pupil darts around, searching not for shapes or people, but for shadows; anywhere the light isn't.

I try to focus on someone near the bed. All I see is a black blur.

"It's too bright. Can we close the curtains?" I plead. "They're already closed," Dad says, voice tight with concern.

My stomach drops. If he's worried, something must be wrong.

"The light is so bright and I can't focus," I say, panic rising.

"It's okay, Owen. Outlines and blurred vision are normal at this stage," says Dr. Simmons.

"How is that okay?" I shoot back.

"Let's move onto the other eye now," he says brushing my comment aside.

I want to scream. I want to throw something. I want to rewind time. But instead, I shut my left eye, letting the brightness fade slightly.

Deep breath.

Same process with the right eye. Same blinding pain. Same indistinct black shapes.

"I can't see!" I yell.

It's like that movie; the one where people get sucked into a TV and everything turns black and white.

Except for me, there's no detail at all.

No clarity.

Just a blur.

A shadow.

A void.

I can hardly take it. In fact, I can't.

My voice is quiet, shaky and almost incoherent as I try to form each word, "Ligh' 'urts my eyes, my visi' is blurred, 'ere's no... 'lour".

"As I said, this will take time," Dr. Simmons replies, more gently now. "But seeing anything at all is a good sign. You'll be given exercises to strengthen your eye muscles. We'll monitor your progress closely here in hospital."

"You don't know if I'll ever see again, do you?" I ask flatly.

Silence.

Then Dad says, "What's happening? Is something wrong with his eyes?"

"Seriously?" I snap. "Isn't it obvious?"

Suddenly, the shadows move closer. I feel their breath. Too close.

Too fast.

Too much.

My heart races. My mind spirals. Is something *really* wrong?

Then— blackness.

Total. Complete. Consuming.

I want the painful light back. Anything but this.

And then...

Doctor Simmons's voice warps into something monstrous.

"You... will... never... see... again. You had... one... chance...

and... you... blew... it."

Then Dad's voice joins in, robotic and haunting: "Never... never... never see again..."

The words echo in my head.

"Nooo!" I cry out. "Please! I have to see! Give me another chance. I promise I'll be better!"

Tears stream down my cheeks. I toss and turn, drowning in the nightmare.

Then—

Gasp.

I bolt upright. In my bed. In my room.

Not the hospital. Not with Dr. Simmons.

Just... home.

It was all a dream.

A nightmare.

Sweat clings to my skin, my sheets soaked.

My breathing is ragged.

My heart is pounding.

It was just a dream. Just a nightmare.

I say it over and over, trying to believe it. But deep down I know...

The nightmare is my reality.

And every day, I still only see shadows.

CHAPTER 8

FIRST DAY OF SCHOOL

I immediately take a shower in an attempt to cool off my body and wash away all the sweat; which would definitely not win me any friends on my first day at a new school.

I know I told Lina I wasn't going, but the nightmare I had last night has made me rethink things. Maybe I *should* try to do better. There's nothing I can do about my vision right now, anyway. At least school will get me out of the house and away from Dad's constant supervision.

Despite the way it ended, it was exhilarating leaving the

house on my own yesterday. I hadn't realised just how much I missed having time to myself. School will give me that. Who's going to want to hang out with the partially blind kid anyway?

* * *

Dad insists on driving me to school; with that same determined tone that makes it pointless to argue. I let him, on the condition that he stays in the car, doesn't toot the horn, and drives away immediately after pointing me to the teacher who's supposed to meet me out front.

This morning in the shower, I felt focused and resolute about returning to school. But now, in the car with the school looming closer, my stomach twists into tiny knots. My palms are like mini ponds— ducks could probably swim in them. In complete contrast, my mouth is dry, like Wanooni's hottest month: November.

"How you doin', kid?" Dad asks.

I let out a grunt, which even surprises me, so I quickly recover.

"Fine, it's just school."

I know he doesn't believe me. He must be noticing my body twitching and jerking in the seat beside him. If not that, then definitely my leg shaking up and down while I try to pin it in place with both hands.

"Yep, it *is* just school. But... it'd be very understandable if you were feeling a bit nervous or even worried," Dad says gently.

"I don't care. I've never cared about school. This isn't going to be any different," I snap.

The car stops. I hear Dad apply the handbrake.

"Okay, here we are," he announces.

We must be at the front of the school. I make out the shape of a large building directly ahead of us; it must be the reception where the teacher said she'd meet me.

"Well, however you are feeling, I hope you have a good day, Owen," Dad says.

Silence fills the car. We both sit there, one hoping the other speaks, the other wishing the day was already over.

And then, as if on cue, Dad breaks the silence again:

"Hmm, yep that's her. She's just come out of the administration building in front of us and she's waving in our direction. Are you sure I can't walk you over?"

"Dad! I can do it. I don't need you holding my hand, I'm twelve," I say, trying to sound confident; even though I am anything but.

I feel for the door handle, pull it, then tentatively swing it open. I rotate my body and cautiously place both feet on the ground, shimmying to feel for a flat stable footing. As I stand, I hear a voice in the distance calling my name.

"She's running. Right at ya," Dad chuckles from inside the car.

I smile a rye smirk at Dad's comment just as a hand clasps my shoulder and a breathless voice reaches my ears.

"Owen?" she asks.

"Yeah. I thought we were meeting at the entrance?" I question, slightly irritated by her over enthusiastic approach.

"Oh yes, I did say that, didn't I? But I saw you sitting in the car and thought I could help you," she says in sing-song voice.

"I'm not completely blind. Or useless," I say firmly.

"Owen, where are your manners?" Dad chimes in.

"It's okay. I can be a bit too eager sometimes. My name's Debbie by the way," she says to Dad.

"Patrick," he replies.

"You can call me Debbie if you like, Owen. Or Ms. Donnington; whatever you are comfortable with," she says.

"Yeah," I mutter, uncertain about this strange woman standing next to me and her *too* bubbly energy. Especially for this small, dumb town.

"Come on then, let me show you around before your first class," says Ms. Donnington.

We spend the next twenty minutes walking in and out of buildings and along paths lined with reflective stickers. They're meant to help people like me navigate the school independently. They'll be installing them on the floors at home too. A great way to single out all the losers, I reckon; just follow the glowing loser path.

Ms. Donnington floats alongside me, her light footsteps matching her voice. I picture her: middle-aged, short brunette hair, matching brown eyes, small build. I don't know if that's true— it's just something I've started doing since the accident. I imagine how people look based on their voices and personalities. One day, I hope to find out if I'm right.

We stop outside what I assume is a classroom. Ms. Donnington calls out, "Toby?"

Footsteps approach. A large shadow fills the doorway. Toby must be huge; tall and wide.

"This is Owen. It's his first day at Wanooni. He's in your class first up," she says.

"Hi Owen, my name is Mr. Peters. Welcome to

Wanooni, and to science. You'll have me first on Mondays and Tuesdays," he says. His voice is surprisingly soft and eager, not what I expected from such a large man. But also, it's like he was complying; he saw me as an inconvenience, someone that needed babysitting in his class.

"I thought my classes were all with you?" I ask Ms. Donnington, disappointed.

"No, sorry, Owen. I only take you for English, History and study periods. You're in mainstream classes for the rest," she explains.

I stand there. Slump. My shoulders drop, my chin almost touching my chest. I wasn't expecting to be with *normal* kids.

"Okay, well... I will see you after science. You've got me next one-on-one for English," says Ms. Donnington, trying to stay upbeat.

* * *

The bell sounds to end Science. I spot a figure at the doorway.

"Hi, Toby," a female voice says. It's Ms. Donnington.

I wish she wouldn't make it so obvious. As if everyone different already notice that I'm the new blind kid. She might as well hold up a neon sign with an arrow pointing at me that says: **'Loser – Pick-up Zone'**.

I drag out packing up my notes, hoping the room clears out before I leave. Mr. Peters made me feel even worse earlier when he said, in front of everyone, "Have a family member read this to you again so you can memorise it." Just because I'm partially blind doesn't mean I'm stupid.

The silence in the room tells me it's mostly empty now. I finish pretending to shuffle things in my bag and sling it over my shoulder.

"How did you go, Owen?" Ms. Donnington asks.

"Easy. I already learnt a lot about space at my old school," I say loudly enough for Mr. Peters to hear.

"That's great. I'm glad there's some crossover. Let me help you out of the classroom— you can follow me to the library. I've booked a room for us to start learning braille," she says cheerfully.

I don't get it. Why bother learning braille? Someone can just read things to me until my vision returns. But I keep those thoughts to myself. I already had this argument with Lina. Her response was like a recording: *It's such a wonderful skill to learn; you'll be glad you did.* I bet Ms. Donnington has listened to that same recording on repeat.

So, I stay quiet and follow her.

She reminds me— again— that the library is at the front of the school and also open to the public.

We enter, take a left, and she opens a squeaky door. Four steps in, she tells me there's a chair to my right. I sit, feel a small round table, and hear her rummaging through her bag.

"Okay, I thought we'd start with something a little different. I'll read you a non-fiction text while guiding your fingers over each braille word. Then I'll ask you some questions about it. Next session, we'll look at the braille alphabet. Sound good?" she asks brightly.

"Yeah. Whatever, I guess," I say.

"Great! So, the title is— let me position your fingers— *Boab Trees.*"

I stand up so quickly from my chair, my head almost explodes with dizziness.

Was she kidding?

Was this some kind of joke?

She must've read my file. She *had* to know.

"What's wrong, Owen?" she asks, as if completely ignorant and in shock by my reaction.

She sounds genuinely confused.

Baffled by me standing here; fuming.

My fists clench. My knuckles turn white. My face must be flaming red. I feel the heat rising from my neck to the tip of my scalp.

Without a word, I storm out; banging my leg on the table as I turn. Five steps out, a turn to the right, and I'm out the library.

It's hard to make a hasty, angry exit when you can't see, but I don't care. I just need to get out.

I don't have a plan for where I am going, but my legs walk as if they do. It's not long before my brain soon catches up.

I'm heading for the corner store.

The main street of Wanooni is like any other rural town. I've only ever lived in places like this, so I could list what's here: a grocery store, the pub/hotel, the doctor's, the cop shop/emergency services, the district high school and library, and of course, a corner store owned by one of the original locals. It has everything you could possibly need, so for those who choose to, there's never a reason to leave.

Some people never do.

Some only leave a few times a year, and never for long. A day.

A weekend.

Me? I want to move to the city as soon as I get my driver's licence and a job. That feels like a lifetime away, especially while I'm stuck here.

I stop in front of the boab tree, just like I did yesterday. I wonder if I'm here to kick it again.

Moments pass. I just stand there, looking up— not with my eyes, because they're no good— but with every other sense I have.

I take in its scent: clean and nostalgic.
I listen.
I feel.
I...

"Back again, are we?" I hear a woman's voice say from behind me.

I can't believe it. It's her; the same woman who was here last time. The one who walked me home. The one who...

"Are you serious? Are you following me or something? Great. You know where I live now too. Go be creepy somewhere else," I say, disgust dripping from my voice.

In a calm tone, she continues, as if completely ignoring what I just said.

"Boabs are special. They…"

"Wow! Lady, seriously, you need to take a hike. I told you; I don't care. Find someone else who actually wants to hear about your stupid tree. You need to get a life," I snap.

"Yes. That's exactly what it's about. Life," she replies gently. "This rude exterior, this wall you put up; it's not who you are. I'm not here to tell you who you are, but I can see you have a connection to this tree. And so do I. I like sharing my story… but I like listening too. Some people aren't ready, and that's okay. But I think you might be. What do you say?"

My response shocks me. I don't know why, but I ask, "What am I ready for?"

"To tell me why you're here," she says.

I don't really know why, but I do. I end up spending the next few hours talking to this complete stranger. I tell her everything— about my first morning at school, about Dad, even about the accident that brought us here.

It feels good.

Talking.

Talking to someone.

Someone who, for the first time in a long time, just…

listens.

CHAPTER 9

STORIES ONCE TOLD

I can't believe I spent the entire afternoon with this stranger.

Except she doesn't feel like one.

I found out her name is Sonia, which doesn't seem right to me. I dunno— doesn't "Sonia" sound like someone who's loud and outgoing? She's quiet and... not. I like that about her. Her personality matches the small shadow I see when I look at her. Without my vision, it's comforting to think there's a link between someone's personality and how they appear to me. I'm only 12 years old, and I'm the same height as her.

I reckon she's around Dad's age, just by the way she talks. She knows lots of fancy words, but she says things in a way I understand. It's like she's been around a while and knows what she's talking about; because she's lived it.

I continue walking home down the street. Sonia walked me to the corner, checked I was okay, and then said she had to go.

I feel light on my feet. I'm not even stressed about stacking it. The loose gravel under the sole of my left foot and the smoothness of the road under my right feel familiar. Talking to Sonia has given me a strange sense of comfort. It was nice, having someone to talk to.

I'm so caught up in my thoughts that I don't even notice the sound of a car slowing behind me until it's right alongside me.

"There you are," says a voice.

Oh no.

It's Dad.

I completely forgot.

Is he just here to pick me up from school?

Was that what we agreed on?

Or worse; did the school call him and tell him that I'd

run out during second session?

"Umm, h-hi," I stammer.

"I thought we agreed I'd pick you up from school," he says, "same place I dropped you off this morning? At least for the first week."

"Oh yeah," I mumble, half-relieved.
Maybe he doesn't know what actually happened today.

"I'm actually pretty impressed you made it this far—on your very first day, I mean. You've got a heck of a memory, kid."

I know he's smiling. I can hear it in the way he says 'kid.'
He hasn't spoken to me like that in a while.

A warm feeling rushes through me. Is Dad... proud of me?

But as quickly as it comes, it's gone; replaced by a pang of guilt.

He doesn't know I didn't even last until recess. He doesn't know I spent the day in town with Sonia. That she helped me walk from town to the beginning of our street. That I've only walked— what?— fifty metres on my own?

"So," Dad says gently, "Do you want me to stay alongside you until we're home, or would you rather walk the rest of the way yourself?"

"Umm… it's been a big day. Can I just get a ride?" I ask.

"O-oh. Of course," Dad stutters, caught off guard by my unusually agreeable tone.

* * *

Mum tucks me into bed tightly.

"As snug as a bug in a rug. Who's my little bug?" she asks, smiling, her eyes drawing me in.

"Muuummm, I'm not your 'bug.' I'm too big to be a bug—I'm six," I say proudly.

"Yes, you are, darling. Which I suppose means you're too big for a bedtime story," she teases.

"No, I'm not!" I reply quickly.

"Okay, okay, Mummy was only teasing. Nobody's ever too big for a story before bed. Even I read before I go to sleep. Now— what story is it going to be tonight?"

"Can I have the story about you again?" I plead.

"Another story about me when I was little?"

"Yeah, I like those ones the best."

"Okay, well let's continue from last night's story, then. Now— where were we?"

"You told me about the time Grandma and Grandpop took you to the crocodile farm. Remember?"

"Oh yes, that's right. Well, that story's finished, so I need to think of a new one. Hmm... how about my tenth birthday?"

"Ooooh, no; you haven't told me that one!" I say, eyes wide.

"Well, it was the morning of my tenth birthday, and I woke up so excited because Grandma and Grandpop had said they had a special surprise for me."

"I'd been telling them for months that I wanted my own horse and to start riding lessons. I was *sure* my birthday present was going to be a horse."

"Was it?" I interrupt.

"You'll just have to wait until I get to that part," she grins.

"Now, I woke up enraptured. I jumped out of bed and ran outside, expecting to see a horse waiting for me. Not just any horse; but a brown one, like the one I rode at the Walshes' farm the spring before."

"I rushed past Grandma and Grandpop in the kitchen and burst through the back door..."

"Was it there?! Did they buy you a horse?" I ask,

bouncing with anticipation.

"There was nothing. Just our backyard, looking the same as always. I felt a bit sad… but then I thought; *maybe* the surprise is that we're going to the stables to pick out my horse."

"So, I bolted back inside, where Grandma and Grandpop were sipping their coffee at the dining table."

"They just looked at me, smiling. 'Happy Birthday,' Grandma said. 'Is everything okay, sweetie?' Grandpop asked.

"That's when I knew; they were pretending. Trying to throw me off. I *was* getting a horse for my birthday."

"Well? Did they take you to the stables?" I ask again, even more impatiently.

Mum chuckles and tells me how they made her favourite breakfast: pancakes with maple syrup and ice cream. Then, keeping with tradition, they measured her height and compared it to the boab tree they planted on the day she was born.

"It was incredible, how much the boab had grown over those ten years…"

"Come on, Mum! Did you get the horse?" I beg.

"To be continued," she says with a sly smile.

"Oh no— Mum, pleeease?"

"You'll just have to wait until tomorrow night."

Mum loved a good cliffhanger. She always said the best books ended their chapters that way; it's what kept people reading. And as much as I begged her to finish her stories, she never did.

Secretly, I liked that most about her stories.

* * *

The alarm shakes me awake. I force my eyes to open as the ringing shrills out, breaking the silence, stating the time is seven am.

My mind is fuzzy, caught between the day and the dream. It felt so real. I hadn't had a dream like that about her before. She felt so close. Like she was still here. I almost expect her to burst through my bedroom door.

But she doesn't.

And she won't.

Because she can't.

It's just another day.

Here. At this house. In this town.

A place I don't want to be.

CHAPTER 10

BLACK HOLE

Miss Donnington walks me to Science in complete silence. I know I should probably apologise for running out on her yesterday, but I don't want to break the silence and make it a big deal.

I reckon she knows it was her fault anyway. Seriously; choosing *that* to read to me? I mean, come on. That's probably why she didn't call Dad to tell him what happened. Probably why she's so quiet now and walking so fast.

I walk through the doorway of the Science room when I feel a gentle hand on my shoulder, holding me back.

"I will pick you up after science. You have history with me, and we need to discuss yesterday's inappropriateness," says Ms. Donnington in a stern tone.

I assume she means *her* inappropriateness. Surely, she doesn't think any of it had to do with me?

"Morning, Owen. Everything okay?" asks Mr. Peters.

"Yeah," I say, brushing him off as I feel my way through the tables and chairs, heading for a seat at the back of the class before anyone else arrives.

"Good, you just looked a bit eh... puzzled," he continues, even though I wish he wouldn't.

"I'm fine," I state sharply, making it clear the conversation is over.

I sit quietly, already wishing it was the end of the day. But it's not. Soon I hear the scuffing of shoes as the Science room begins to fill up, followed by the loudspeaker version of Mr. Peters' voice.

"Settle down now. We're going to begin. Anyone who doesn't might find themselves in... today's topic, which is... black holes."

He laughs his best evil laugh.

"I'll be giving you a quiz on it at the end of the session. Don't worry, Owen, I'll read you the questions and get you to tell me your answers verbally," shout-whispers Mr. Peters, leaning over my desk.

Great. Just what I need; special attention. As if being the new blind kid wasn't enough, now I apparently need everything repeated like I'm dumb *and* deaf.

Then I notice two kids, or at least two shadows, sitting at the front of the room. I can feel them staring at me. The screeching sound their chairs make as they turn around gives them away. They must be trying to hear what Mr. Peters is saying to me. I can just imagine their empathetic faces, feeling sorry for me. It's not me they should be feeling sorry for.

Losers, I think.

"Okay, who can tell me something they know about black holes? Yes, Derek?" says Mr. Peters.

"Well, there are two types of black holes. There are the Supermassive black holes and then the Stellar black holes, which are the most common. Scientists think that one day humans might be able to use black holes to time travel forward," says the Derek kid, giggling.

What a dweeb, I think.

Definitely one of the ones who was staring at me.

"Yes, well done, Derek. Good knowledge," praises Mr.

Peters.

"What an absolute nerd," I mutter under my breath' or so I thought.

"Something you would like to add, Owen?" asks Mr. Peters.

"Nope," I say folding my arms and leaning back in my seat.

"Don't be shy. I remember you said you learnt a lot about space at your old school," he adds cheerily.

That must be a dig at me for yesterday's comment. Please, just stop picking on me.

"I don't want to," I reply gruffly.

"That's okay. But next time, I'd like you to share, please. Now, let's talk about the most common black holes, like Derek said, Stellar Mass. They form when massive stars implode at the end of their life cycle. After it's formed, the black hole can grow by absorbing mass from its surroundings. Its gravitational pull is so strong that nothing can escape- not even light."

Mr. Peters continues, but his voice fades away. My thoughts take over.

Black holes sound like my life.

Sometimes I get so angry I feel like I might implode.

Like I'm trapped; a lump of mass that can't escape, no matter how much I try.

Can't escape this body that doesn't work. That doesn't see.

Can't escape my dad, who doesn't let me do anything.

Can't escape this school full of strangers.

Can't escape my thoughts of her.

And because I can't escape, everything closes in around me. I'm left with all this extra stuff that makes me want to implode all over again.

And while all that pressure builds, time feels like it stops.

I'm not really living; I'm just existing.

Waiting.

But I don't even know what I'm waiting for.

"Okay, it's quiz time! Voices off from now, please," says Mr. Peters.

Oh no. I've missed the entire lesson.

How did that even happen?

This isn't good. It's going to be so embarrassing.

I'm going to have to give my answers *out loud,* and everyone will think I'm some dumb kid who can't keep up.

I want to run. Heat rises up my neck. My stomach twists. I think I'm going to be sick.

"Are you okay, Owen?" asks Mr. Peters, sounding concerned.

I snap out of it. "Yeah," I respond hoarsely.

"You sure? You walked in this morning looking a little... then during class I noticed... and now you look..." He trails off. "Are you okay?"

I shrug, and before I realise it, my head drops forward, my elbows land on the desk, and my hands cover my face.

"It's okay, Owen. Well, maybe it's *not,* and that's why I don't want to push you. If you just want to chill for the last few minutes, I'll let you. *This time,* at least. Don't expect it going forward— we can't have you falling behind," says Mr. Peters sympathetically.

I hate that tone; like he feels sorry for me.

But right now, I'm just grateful I don't have to do the quiz.

So I let it go and slump further into my seat, waiting for the day to end.

The bells rings. I'm more than happy to leave. I don't even wait for the room to clear; I just stand and make my way around the edge of the room toward the door.

"Until next time, Owen," Mr. Peters calls.

I step out, take a few steps, and then realise I have no clue where I'm going. Debbie is supposed to meet me to take me to history. I don't know if it's in the library again or somewhere else. Honestly, I don't think I could even find the library on my own.

Yesterday at school was a blur.

I step to one side of the door and; *Thud!*

My shoulder blade smacks into something.

"I'm so sorry; are you okay?" says a soft voice.

I turn toward the figure standing close to me. Hard to make anything out, but with that voice, it's definitely a girl. "I'm sorry. I'm Jo. Are you okay?" she repeats.

It must look like I'm staring. Maybe she's wondering if something's wrong.
Didn't they say the new kid was partially blind— not completely mute?

Finally, I manage a weak, "Hi."

She takes a step back just as another figure approaches; shorter than both of us.

"Hi, I'm Derek," he says.

Oh, great. These must be the nerds from the front of class. Or... maybe just her? I'm not sure.

"So, we obviously have science together," Jo says, "but I

didn't see you in any of my other classes yesterday. Maybe we have history or..."

"Are you a creeper?" I interrupt, trying to sound cool.

"She was just being nice," Derek says defensively.

That irritates me. I wasn't talking to *him*. Just wish he'd go away.

"Did I ask you, Nerd? Shouldn't you be running off to make sure you get the seat closest to the front in your next class?" I snap, hoping to impress Jo.

"We were just being nice. We were going to tell you about Goalball, but I don't think it's a good idea anymore. Come on, Derek," Jo says with a bit of sass that wasn't there before.

I smirk. She put me in my place. Used a basic FOMO strategy, and it worked.

"Go on— Goalball. What even is that?" I ask.

There's a pause, like she's deciding if she even wants to tell me.

"You haven't heard of Goalball before? Really? Well, it's a game where you try to roll a ball with bells into the opponent's net to score points. The other team stays on their hands and knees and uses ear-hand coordination to block the shots. You might have to wear blackout glasses, depending on your vision."

"That's a sport? Doesn't sound like one. They're on their hands and knees? That's pathetic," I scoff.

"Hi, Owen— sorry I'm late," says Ms. Donnington, arriving beside me. "I'm glad Joanne and Derek kept you company. Don't let me interrupt you talking to your friends."

"We're done. And we're not friends. Let's go," I say, annoyed.

The only reason Jo talked to me was probably to use me—thought I had some kind of advantage. That because I can't see, I must have super senses or something.

Like I must be used to it.

Not a chance, and I never will.

I won't have to.

I'll be seeing properly again soon.

Even as I think it, I know I don't believe it.

CHAPTER 11

THE NAGGING QUESTION

Longest. Day. Ever.

This morning, I told Dad I wanted to walk home by myself again, just like yesterday. He was too preoccupied by his own thoughts, probably about work, to question or protest.

I'm currently regretting that decision. Right now, I just want to be home. I suppose it's my first proper full day back at school since the accident, which was months ago.

I think even Ms. Donnington could see how exhausted I was during the last session of the day. I didn't complain or say anything when she told me off for storming out on her yesterday. She said it was inappropriate behaviour, and if I did it again, she'd have to consider calling my dad. I just nodded, which is probably why— fifteen minutes before the final bell— she gave me a head start and let me leave early.

Of course, it came with strict instructions to walk straight home, and that she would need to walk me to the front of the school.

I didn't mind.

The hardest part for me is walking *through* the school. Not because I'm partially blind, but because I'm still trying to find my way around. It's not a big school, but it's laid out in a really strange way. You'd think the primary and high school classrooms would be in separate sections, but everything's kind of jumbled together. Like, the Year 3/4 classroom is right next to the Science room, which is only used by high school students. And the Pre-Primary rooms are right beside the Home Economic rooms for the seniors specialising in hospitality. It's weird.

"Now make sure you follow through on your promise, Owen. Straight home, yeah?" Ms. Donnington says.

"Yes. Well, kinda. I need to stop at the shop before I go home. We're out of bread. Dad's been so busy with his work, I thought I'd show him I can help around the house," I lie.

I hope she doesn't realise how ridiculous that sounds coming from someone with impaired vision.

We've got plenty of bread at home. I just want to go past the corner store so I can walk by the boab tree. I don't know why; I just want to sit under it for a bit before heading home.

"Oh. Okay, that isn't too much of a detour, I suppose. And you have got time, it's only ten to three," says Ms. Donnington, already out of breath from walking a few meters. I can tell she doesn't get much exercise.

"Thanks. See you tomorrow," I say, way too cheerily.

"No worries, Owen. Take care," she calls out.

But I'm already upping my pace, speeding up, as I head down the path leading out of school.

* * *

I feel the low-hanging branches, and can tell it's beginning to lose its leaves; just like it's supposed to this time of year. Soon its starkness will be revealed, and only the true form of the tree will remain. I slump down next to it, resting my back against the strong, thick trunk.

The barrenness of the boab, once it's shed its leaves, can make it seem weak or ugly.

But I think the opposite is true.

Its beauty is why so many artists paint it, why photographers come during the dry season just to capture it.

It's not weak— it just changes, adapting to survive its environment.

We all do that in some way.

Geez, I'm starting to sound just like *her*.

These facts spill out of me like some kind of nature documentary. I probably know more about boabs than anything else.

She told me everything.

I needed this after today— just to sit, just to *be* here.

But I can't stay. I need to get home before Dad starts to freak out. I slowly get to my feet, drawing in one deep breath before exhaling it, when I see the petite outline of a figure, I think I know.

"Sonia?" I ask.

"Yes, it's me. Hello, Owen. We're starting to make a habit of this—bumping into each other at the corner store. Picking something up?" she asks, even though she knows that's not why I'm here.

"No, I was just on my way home from school and took a wrong turn. But I know where I am and how to get home," I say, not wanting to admit I came here just to sit under the boab.

"Was school better today?" Sonia asks.

"Yeah. Well... I made it through the whole day," I laugh.

"I'd say that's a good day then. Did you learn anything or meet anyone interesting? That would make it a great day," she adds playfully.

"Um... we learned about black holes in Science, I guess. And I met these two people in class, but I don't think they're that interesting. They just want me to play this silly sport because of my vision," I tell her.

"I'd say that's a *great* day! Black holes are wondrous, wouldn't you say?" she says, amused.

"I guess," I mutter.

"I mean, when you think about it; it's like a stunning reincarnation of life. One ends— the star— and another begins— the black hole. The star itself was amazing, but the black hole is a new, different entity. It doesn't think back to what it *was*, it just *is*. It *has* to be, to survive. Don't you think, Owen?"

"Yeah, I suppose so," is all I can manage.

I don't really understand what she's talking about. But I get this feeling; like I did the first time I met her. I think... she's trying to say something. Not with her words, but in the way she says them. I can't figure it out, but it's there, nagging at me.

"I'm sure if you get to know Derek and Jo, they could be good friends. You can't really know how interesting someone is after just one conversation, can you?" Sonia says.

I turn toward the boab and think back to my chat with Derek and Jo earlier.

But that's just a distraction.

What I really feel is this strange sense of wonder and unease. Something's off.

I turn back toward her.

But she's gone.

"Sonia?" I call out.

Silence.

"Sonia?" I say again, more desperately.

But she's vanished. It's like, one minute she was here and the next... gone.

I can't shake these strange feelings that are starting to build up around her. The questions I want to ask. Like, why is she *always* here? I think back to my first day— driving into town. Even then, I'm sure I saw her standing by the boab.

Does she have a family?

A job?

Why didn't she say something to Dad that night at the house, when we first met?

Why didn't she tell him what she saw me do to the tree?

What is it about her that calms me?

But the thing that eats at me the most; the question that started all this:

How did she know?

How did she know their names were Derek and Jo?

CHAPTER 12

THE DECISION - WE'RE MOVING

I reach the steps of my front porch and press my watch. It drones out the time: *three twenty-one.* That's good, I think to myself, knowing Dad would have expected me home around now.

As I look down at the first step, preparing myself to gauge its height once more, I notice that each one has reflective stickers– just like the ones at school on all the paths. Having them on the stairs outlines each step perfectly, letting me judge the depth much easier.

A sense of dread creeps over me as I realise this must

mean Lina was here today. I cross my fingers, hoping she's already come and gone, and make my way up the stairs with ease. Slowly, as if I am a thief in the night checking for unlocked doors, I twist the handle of the front door and attempt to open it quietly- but I'm unsuccessful. The door lets out a loud squeak.

With my plan foiled, I step over the small footing without any care and follow the reflective strip along the hallway toward the kitchen. I get there in no time— whether it's the stickers making things quicker or just my stomach growling, I'm not sure. But for the first time, things seem a little easier.

I'm starving.

I hear the television on as I enter the room but ignore it, focused only on the fridge. I pause with my hand on the handle, ready to pull it open, when it hits me: it's not even three-thirty, and Dad has the TV on.

What is going on?

He never has it on when he's working.

We've had so many arguments about me doing homework in front of the TV. He always says, *there's no way you're doing your homework properly with that thing on. And if you are, it'll take you twice as long.*

Something doesn't feel right.

My stomach grumbles again, and I let out a sigh. Then, hesitantly, I call out, "Hi Dad, are you in here?"

"Yep. Here I am," he says in what sounds like an annoyed tone, coming from the direction of the couch.

He must be in one of his moods. I know I should tread carefully, but then again, it usually doesn't make a difference. It hasn't in the past. So, I press on.

"Are you working this afternoon?"

"Nope," he replies sharply.

Another clear warning: *Don't push it.* But like Mum, I can't let things go. I wonder what could've happened today. There's nothing special this month. No appointments. No scheduled visits.

Did it have something to do with Lina?

The stickers on the front steps and the floor throughout the house tells me someone was definitely here today.

"Did Lina come today?" I ask.

"Yep," he replies quickly.

The TV's audio changes. It sounded like a fishing show before.

Bait, lure, gaff, jigging.

I know all those words from the times we used to go fishing

together. It's been a long time. I miss it.

Dad would pretend to be annoyed when we got home because I'd tell Mum I caught the biggest fish, while he had to throw most of his back; they were too small. That was before. Before everything happened. Things will never be the same again.

Now it sounds like a cooking show; one of those with the overly energetic host trying to make cooking seem more fun than it really is.

Mum never liked cooking. She used to say she was glad she wasn't born in the days of doing everything from scratch—because even putting something in the oven for fifteen minutes was too much for her.

My stomach growls again. I decide it's best to end this conversation with a nothing statement.

"Okay then."

He clearly doesn't want to talk, and there's definitely something going on. But I don't want this to turn into one of our massive fights. Hunger wins. I grab a few things from the fridge and head to my room. I don't want to spend another second in that room— it feels like a bomb is strapped to it, counting down to detonation.

* * *

Knock. Knock.

"Can I come in, Owen?" Dad asks from outside my bedroom door.

He pushes it open before I can even answer. I'm lying on top of my bed and don't bother sitting up.

I'm still annoyed.

With him.

With the situation.

With everything.

"There's something we have to talk about," he says.

"Yeah," I reply, not really wanting to hear it.

"We've been out of the hospital for over a week now. We need to start making some of the changes Doctor Simmons talked about. It's all about making things easier for you," he adds.

"Easier? Pfft, sure," I scoff.

"I know... I know you were strongly against it in the hospital when Doctor Simmons suggested it, but... we are going to--- we *need* to move."

"What? We don't need to move!" I shout.

"I've bought a property in Wanooni. The one with the really good school for kids like you. I've started making arrangements with Lina to prepare the house in order to..."

I shoot to my feet so fast the blood rushes from my head. I feel like I might fall, but instead I lose something else—

My temper.

My mind.

"You've *got* to be kidding. You already bought a house? You've already gone behind my back? Do I even get a say?" I rage.

"Owen, sometimes a parent has to make decisions for their child— not based on what they *want*, but what they *need*. This is one of those decisions."

"Oh, is it just? One of *your* decisions got us here in the first place. And *that* decision definitely wasn't in the best interest of your child!"

He stands silent.

Only now do I realise how close I am to him— because I can hear it.

His sniffling.

His heavy breathing.

You'd think that would stop me. But I'm too far gone.

"It should have been you," I cry.

Silence.

Now it's only my breathing— short, sharp, uneven. The room feels drained of light. Time feels like it's stopped. I think I might collapse or curl up on the floor when—

He turns and walks away. At the doorway, he pauses.

"I'm putting the house up for sale this week. We move at the end of the month," he says evenly, then quietly shuts the door behind him.

I can hear my heart pounding in my chest, like a frog trapped in a cookie jar, banging against the lid, trying to escape.

My breathing's heavy. I focus: in through the nose, out through the mouth— like the psychologist taught me.

One of the coping strategies.

She said I'd need it.

Not *if*, but *when*.

Was this a panic attack?

My legs wobble beneath me. I jostle back toward the bed before they give way. I fall onto the mattress, bracing myself with sweaty hands.

I sit.

Elbows on knees.

Fists clenched.

Head bowed.

I don't move.

I wait.

I wait for my heartbeat to slow.

I wait for my breathing to settle.

I wait.

Just... wait.

My eyes twitch under closed lids, my hands scrunch the sheets beside me. Slowly, my heartbeat returns to normal. My breath steadies. I realise my eyes are filled with tears.

I must've fallen asleep after coming back to my room with snacks.

I've tried so hard to forget that time— in our old house— when I said those things to Dad.

I lost control.

Of everything.

It still haunts me. In my waking hours, and especially when I sleep.

The guilt tears me awake.

Just another nightmare from the real one I'm still living.

I sit upright.

I think about yesterday afternoon.

Why was Dad watching TV instead of working?

Did he fight with Lina?

I don't know.

I've never really seen him cry.

He doesn't cry.

He just gets into those moods— like yesterday.

Well, once, I heard him cry at the hospital. He didn't think anyone was listening.

I think it was about *her.*

I lie back down.

Waiting.

My eyes are wide open, but all I see is darkness. No light. No shadows. Just black.

Sometimes, I think maybe this would be better.

I press my watch. It drones again: *three twenty-one.*

I know I need a few more hours of sleep before I have to get up.

It's going to be another long day.

CHAPTER 13

SOMEONE I ONCE KNEW

I don't even take my first step onto the school grounds before I know I am in for it.

"Hey!" she shouts.

Even before she's standing right in front of me, her shadowed face less than an arm's length away, I know it's Jo. And she's not happy. I'm guessing this is about yesterday, with her and Derek.

She's doing a whole lot of yelling right now, but I'm not really listening to what she is saying. I'm focused on her shadowed features, her tone, her voice. It's hard to notice all those things when you can physically see. I never used to pay attention. But when you're partially blind, you learn to zoom in on someone's characteristics.

They call them idiosyncrasies; the little things that make someone unique. I've gotten pretty good at identifying people from a distance, just by how they carry themselves. Their voice mostly, but also their shape. It can be tricky, lots of people have similar builds. But if you look closely, there's always something distinct.

Take Jo, for instance. She has a petite, slender body, but unusually broad shoulders for her size. Maybe she swims or...

"Are you even listening to me, Owen?" she snaps.

"Oh, umm... no. Sorry," I admit.

Damn. That's the one problem with taking in mental notes, I get caught out not listening. How do I get out of this? Maybe I can use my impairment to my advantage for once. "Who are you? I can't see."

"Don't play that card with me, Owen. You know exactly who I am. We had a whole conversation yesterday. A rude one. But it still happened. It's Jo. And remember Derek? The guy you were rude to the other day? Ringing any bells?"

She looks like she is standing up on her tip toes now,

trying to be taller, but I'm still taller. It's like she is trying to be menacing, her hands placed on her hips, making her silhouette wider.

"Are you standing on your tip toes?" I ask.

"What? I'm just stretching my ankles. They're weak. That's not the point. Wait... how did you know I was on my tiptoes?" she asks, baffled.

"Don't worry. I'm still blind, if that's what you're worried about. But only partially, you know. I'm very good at outlines, movement, figures, voices, tones... and I even know when someone's smiling," I say modestly.

It's quiet for a moment while she processes that.

"How do I look to you?" Jo asks sheepishly, clearly hoping for a polite answer.

She doesn't need to worry. Despite the ambush, I feel calm and oddly at ease talking to her.

"Well... I can see that you're quite small. I mean, petite. Girls look good— uh, I mean, being petite is okay for girls. You like to use your hands a lot when you speak, or put them on your hips. Especially when you're telling someone off."

I grin, knowing I'm right, and she knows it too.

"But I've only spoken to you twice now. I'm sure I'll

pick up on more--- stuff that's unique to you. You know, the more we chat," I say, trying to impress her but stay cool at the same time.

"Okay, yeah. Anyway, I just wanted to say you were really rude to Derek yesterday. He's nice. You shouldn't talk to people like that, especially not Derek."

"Yeah, I know. I wasn't having a good morning. Plus Mr. Peters was picking on me in science. You were there; you must've heard him."

"He wasn't picking on you. He was just trying to make sure you felt included," Jo says.

"Included? I don't think so," I reply sharply.

"Okay, if you say so. And another thing— we weren't being rude when we asked you to play Goalball. We just thought you might like to meet some new people. You know, since you've just moved here. Ms. Donnington said you played soccer at your old school, so I figured you'd like other sports too. You'll love Goalball. I promise."

"So let me get this straight; you've been talking to Ms. Donnington about me?" I say in my best impression of a stern voice.

"Oh... umm... I wasn't—"

"Relax. I'm just teasing," I say with a smile.

She laughs, but I can't tell if it's a real laugh or one of those polite, awkward ones people give when they think you're a bit weird.

So, I try again. "And just what did Ms. Donnington say about me— besides the fact that I was the star football player at my old school?"

"Oh, you know. The usual stuff. That you're full of yourself and wouldn't be a very good teammate for Goalball," she says, cheekily.

"Oh, did she now? Yet here you are, begging me to play," I say.

"Yeah. Oh, I'm sorry, maybe I wasn't clear before. I want you to play *against* us. I want to be on the team that *smashes* your team."

She lets out a little snort, then bursts into laughter, and so do I. That's when I know: her laugh is genuine. She's just trying to be nice.

Trying to be my friend.

* * *

"How was your day?" Sonia asks, standing under the boab.

"I thought you might be here," I say.

"Were you looking for me?"

"No," I reply, unconvincingly.

"It's okay, you can tell me, you know. Did something happen? At school? At home?"

Sonia's so kind and caring, I feel like I can tell her anything. I lean with my back against the boab's massive trunk, facing her.

"It was actually a good day... though it didn't start that way. Yesterday I was pretty horrible to these two kids. Derek and Jo. Mostly Derek. They were telling me about Goalball and... well, I wasn't very nice."

"Oh. But today you were... nicer?" she asks, gently but firmly. "You know you should treat others the way you want to be treated."

I turn to face the tree and run my open hands along the enormous trunk.

"I was nicer. You know, that's what my mum always said? But she'd somehow link it to a boab tree," I say, chuckling at the memory.

"Well, sounds like she was a wise lady."

My eyes drop to my feet.

"She was."

Sonia changes the subject. "Now, what is this Goalball?

I've never heard of it."

I glance up at the boab again, and for the first time, notice how close the corner store is to its branches.

"That makes two of us. Jo invited me to check it out. She reckons I'll *love* it."

"But you're not so sure?" Sonia asks, reading my mind.

"It doesn't *sound* like a real sport. And I love playing football. As soon as I recover, I'll be back at it. So, what's the point?"

I feel her arm brush against mine as she moves closer.

"Yeah, okay. But in the meantime, you could still have fun playing Goalball. Meet new people. Make some friends. Who knows— you might even like it more than soccer. And it's important to play *something*."

I start walking slowly around the base of the boab, balancing carefully, feeling the soil and bark underfoot.

"Yeah, I suppose. I'll think about it."

"There's no harm in checking it out. If you don't like it, at least you'll know for sure."

I stop and look toward her.

"You know, normally I'd get angry when someone tells me what to do. But somehow, you get away with it. How does that work?"

"It's what I do. I've always done it," she says, her voice suddenly distant.

I continue around the back of the tree.

"You know, the other day I turned around and you were just... gone. You've done that before, too. I was actually going to ask you something. Can I ask you now?"

Silence.

I make my way back around to the front of the boab.

"Sonia? I can see you standing there. You haven't disappeared this time... Sonia?"

I call her name again, and again— but I'm met with silence.

And then, suddenly, I hear a *man's* voice: "Are you okay?"

"Yes, I'm just talking to her," I say, pointing at Sonia.

But when I turn... she's gone.

"What the—? She was right here. She disappeared again. I swear she was here. Her name's Sonia," I plead, needing him to believe me.

"Wait, who are you?" I ask. "Where did you come from?"

"My name's Sam. I own the corner shop over there. Look, I don't know anyone named Sonia around here. Do you want me to call someone?" he asks, sounding worried in a way I've grown used to over the past few months.

"No. I'm just on my way home. I'm fine," I say, deflated.

I decide it's time to head home. And the whole way back, I'm haunted by a feeling I can't shake.

CHAPTER 14

GOALBALL

All the way here I kept thinking to myself: *What am I doing? Turn around and go home. Why am I even thinking about this? I don't want to go there.*

I don't owe Jo, and definitely not Derek, anything.

And yet, my feet kept walking while my mind kept doubting.

Maybe I was trying to convince myself I didn't want to go, but that wasn't true. What I really wanted was to make friends— and going to Goalball was a way of doing that.

I wanted to play a sport. And at the moment, that sport couldn't be football. But I knew it had to be something. Something with a team. Teammates. I missed that the most. Well, at least how it was in the beginning with my old team. When Dad would come, and actually watch me play. And Mum— she'd be there too, sipping on a can of soft drink, cheering me on.

I know this wouldn't be like that. But... what if it could be a little like that?

All this thinking I've been doing, and yet here I am, standing out the front of the Goalball centre— and I didn't once think about how I was going to check it out without anyone seeing me. Or without me being able to see.

Sometimes I can be really dumb.

Jo told me all the details the other day at school. She was so casual about it, like we'd known each other for years. Like I'd already said yes to coming. Not the reality, which was, I told her I'd *think* about it.

I was walking with Ms. Donnington on my way to the library for English. I could tell Jo was coming towards us. Those broad shoulders, petite frame, and her voice. She was talking with some other girls. Friends, I guess. The passageway can get quite busy between classes, but I could pick out her voice and her laugh above everything else. She was laughing— at herself, I think. Letting her friends laugh at her just as much.

As we got closer, I could sense she was heading straight towards me, right up against the highlighted sticker path— meant only for people like me. Then, just as I thought we were about to collide, I stupidly closed my eyes, waiting, expecting...
But all I felt was the slightest brush of our upper arms touching.

Clearly, she knew just how to move to the side of the blind kid, while I, being the idiot, just kept walking.

Seconds passed, and I turned around. She noticed and called out to me:

"Hey Owen! Don't forget— four o'clock on Thursday at Wanooni Rec Centre. I'll see you there!"

I didn't get angry or annoyed. I just smiled like a weirdo and said, "Okay."
I don't even know why.

Usually, I get so irritated by people being pushy and telling me what to do.
But just like the other day with Sonia, I was fine with it.
Even happy she asked me.

* * *

"Gather around," boomed a man's voice.

I quickly made my way along the side of the building. A cool sensation hit my arm as I gently leaned against the wall. It was glass; a window. I shuffled slightly to the left, so I wasn't pressing against it anymore. Didn't want to be seen.

"Okay, welcome to Goalball. I'm Coach Cardiff. Let's see, how many do we have? One, two, three, four, five, six, seven, eight. Joanne? Did you say you had someone else for your team?" he asked.

"Yeah... but doesn't look like he's coming," I heard her reply, her voice a little deflated.

"That's okay. We have a few options with eight, and we've got a couple of weeks until the tournament begins, so not to worry."

I felt bad. I wanted to run in there. Tell them I was sorry for being late. But my feet felt heavy, like they were glued to the ground. I couldn't move.

I shouldn't feel bad. I didn't say I was definitely coming. I just wanted to check it out first. See for myself. I wasn't sure if I really wanted to play.

Coach Cardiff continued:
"Now, one of the most important things to know about

Goalball is that it's an ear-hand coordination sport. For many of you, this is not something you've trained your body to do before. It's tricky. Some people just find it too difficult to play. So, if you don't like a challenge, this sport's not for you."

This is exactly what I've trained my body to do.

"The other thing— you've got to be okay diving around on a hard court. Despite the padding, it can hurt. You'll go home with bruises."

No more than from football.

"Also, you need to listen very carefully when I teach you about the court layout— so you know where to position yourself and avoid crashing into teammates. It doesn't matter if you're completely, partially, or not blind at all— everyone must wear blacked-out eye shades. That way, visibility is the same for every player. Any questions so far?"

Wow. This actually sounded kind of cool.

The recreation centre was a large, open building with windows that let the light pour in. Really bright. I'd have needed to block it out anyway, so the eye shades would be good for me.

I'd be killer at this sport.

I already do so much ear-hand coordination stuff— I'd

be steps ahead of the others. Especially Derek and Jo.

I wondered. Are there any other kids in there who are like me? Or completely blind?

If there were, they'd go to Wanooni District too, same as me. I would've met them by now. Wouldn't I?

I squashed the thought the moment it hit me. Disappointment followed fast.

I shook myself, tuned back in.

"Yes, Derek, isn't it?" asked Coach Cardiff.

Of course, Derek had a question.

Coach's pet *and* teacher's pet.

"Is it true that to play Goalball at the Paralympics, you have to have a vision impairment?" he asked.

"Yes. But we're not at the Paralympics, are we, Derek?" the coach replied.

Wow, I thought. *I could play Goalball at the Paralympics. Win a gold medal.*

If I got really good... I could actually do that.

"Do you have another question, Derek?"

"Yes. How do you score a goal?"

"That's a good question. As you know, the ball has to be thrown a particular way, otherwise, you might give away possession. We'll get into speed balls, curve balls, all that later. But it's really about the tactics. I'll let everyone have a go at throwing today so I can figure out who fits best in centre or wing positions. Hopefully, we'll get some blocking practice in too— for our more defensive players."

I'd be awesome at defence. Blocking shots. Reading the play. Like I did in football.

And my shots would be pretty good too— I'd have a mean curve ball.

Jingle. Jingle. Jingle.

"This is the ball," said Coach Cardiff. "As you can hear, it's got bells inside. That's so you can hear where it is at any moment in the match. Like I said before, it's a sport of ear-hand coordination.

"Okay, that's enough talk. Everyone grab a ball and let's get shooting! Don't worry about the other equipment, we're purely focused on technique."

I wanted to grab a ball. I wanted to join in. But I knew I had to go.

I'd heard enough. I knew what I wanted to do. What I *was* going to do.

There was only one thing standing in my way.

Dad.

CHAPTER 15

A KALEIDOSCOPE OF COLOURS

I get home from Goalball and leap up the stairs of the front porch without even thinking– no checking, no stopping. It's as if I've done it a million times before, and my feet know what to do even before my eyes have had a chance to calculate or worry.

I am home.

I hear Dad in the kitchen. It can only be him, the way the cupboards are being slammed shut. He's not angry; he's just a notorious door-slammer, as Mum used to say.

I remember when I was little, lying in bed in the mornings,

listening to Dad getting ready for work.

I'd know when he was reaching for his teapot by the way he'd groan as he bent down, then the cupboard door would slam shut, like he was in the biggest hurry. He only ever cared about making sure the door was closed, not about doing it quietly.

Then came the running water as he filled the kettle, the click of the switch being turned on, and the clatter of condiments and jars in the fridge door as he opened and shut it with the same force.

His hurried steps over the creaking floorboards echoed as he walked from the kitchen to the couch. Then, finally, there'd be a moment of quiet while he sipped his tea.

Mum used to get so irritated by it all. She'd say, *'Hey Door Slammer, could you be any louder?'*

Dad would roll his eyes and say she was 'hyper-sensitive,' all because she was trying to catch those last few minutes of sleep before I woke up.

Of course, that would get Mum going, and it would start this back-and-forth of mock name-calling. Not a fight— something different, warmer. A loving, laughing, competitive match until one of them said something so ridiculous they'd both end up in fits of laughter.

"Hi Dad," I say as I walk past the kitchen on my way to the couch. I haven't spent much time in the TV room since the accident— for obvious reasons. Me sitting on the couch now says, *I want to talk*, which is strange. Because I don't ever *just* want to talk.

Dad knows that if I come home and go straight to my room, I want to be left alone. He'll still come in sometimes to talk, but he knows how that usually ends.

"Hi Owen, did you have fun with your friends this afternoon?"

"Yeah, it was okay," I say.

"You know, I don't mind if you want to invite your friends over here. Just give us a couple of weeks to settle in first."

"We were just hanging out at the rec, not at anyone's house," I say casually, wondering why he suddenly wants people to come over.

"Oh, okay. Is that where all the cool kids hang out these days?" he asks, using his most embarrassingly dorky voice.

I roll my eyes. "Nah, not really."

"I'm just making a snack. Want something?"

I shake my head. Then I feel the shift of the couch as he sits beside me.

"I know you said you were meeting some friends this

afternoon, but you didn't say who," he says, trying to keep it casual while also fishing for information.

"Just a couple of people from school," I say, knowing this answer will only spark more questions.

"Oh yeah? That's great you've met people so quickly. Where'd you first meet them?"

"School."

"Haha, you know what I mean."

"They're in my science class."

"I used to love science. The experiments. Bunsen burners, all that. So good. What are you learning about now?"

"Black holes. We haven't done any experiments yet. Not like at my old school," I say, annoyed.

"What are your friends' names?" he asks, smoothly switching topics.

"Derek and Jo. Well, really only Jo," I clarify.

"Oh, okay. And what's Jo like? Is he the kind of boy a dad would want his son hanging around with?"

"Nope," I say, smirking.

"Why not?" he asks, concerned.

"Because Jo is a girl, Dad. Joanne. Jo is short for Joanne."

"Oh! Haha. You really never know these days, do you?" he chuckles.

Dad seems to be in a good mood today. I think to myself, *It's now or never.*

"So, Dadddd?"

"Yeahhhhhh," he says, mimicking my tone. He knows I'm about to ask for something.

I take a deep breath.

"I want to get back into playing sport again."

"Oh yeah, absolutely. Sport is important. As soon as you're ready, when you've recovered, we can look into what's available here."

"No, I mean— I want to play sport *now.*"

"Owen... you're not... you *can't* play sport at the moment."

"Why won't you even listen to what I have to say? You never listen. You just tell me what I can and can't do all the time."

"Because I'm your dad, and I know what's best for you."

My fists clench.

My chewed-down nails dig into my palms.

I feel the heat rising up my neck. My breathing gets heavy.

Why does he always have to be this way?

He never understands.

What I want.

What I need.

"I'm telling you; I *can* play sport!" I yell.

"I'm sorry, Owen. I know you want to, but it's not possible right now. There are lots of reasons- not just your sight. One of them is that I don't have the time, with my job, to take you to and from games and training."

His words make my blood boil. Lies.

"You don't have to take me. I don't need you. I can get there myself. Mum didn't take me either, but at least she *came to watch.*
I want her here. It's your fault she's not. Why couldn't you?"

I stop myself. The words burn at the back of my throat. Tears sting behind my eyes like a volcano ready to erupt, but I refuse to let them.

I stand abruptly and take a few steps toward the hallway. I have to leave.
I have to get out before I say something I'll regret.

Then he says it. The words I've been dreading. The ones I've repeated in my head for months, except this time, they're not my thoughts.
They're his.

"She wasn't supposed to be there."
"Who?" I shout, turning around.

"Your mum."

"What do you mean?"

"In that spot. The backseat. She wasn't meant to be there...
You were," he says.

There it is. Confirmation of what I've always known but
never wanted to hear.

It *was* my fault.

I clutch the doorframe. The dizziness hits like a wave.
My legs weaken. My grip tightens.

Short, shallow breaths. I'm panicking.

The room spins in black and white shapes like some warped
illusion.

I fixate on one spot, trying to ground myself.

Then, a flash.

Bright and sudden, like a camera in the dark.

Then again.

And again.

Like it's on a timer.

But the last one is different. A burst of colour— strange,
swirling colours. Random, but beautiful.

I can see.

Colour. For the first time since the accident.

I slide down the doorframe, no longer angry, just...

amazed.

I land hard, but I don't care.

I turn my head, trying to take it all in.

I must look insane— like someone frantically searching for something precious.

Which, I guess... I am.

And everywhere I look, there it is— *colour.*

My lips curve into a smile.

This is it!

My sight is coming back!

I hear Dad in the background say something. Maybe 'sorry,' maybe 'what's going on?'— but I ignore him.

Then the colours change.

They begin to fade. Darken.

Red becomes brown.

Blue becomes navy.

Then black.

I search for more colour, turning my head rapidly.

But it's all gone.

Black again.

Just shadows.

All of it. Gone.

Only the darkness remains.

CHAPTER 16

SURVIVAL

The wet season has been particularly violent this year. The monsoonal, hot and humid weather typical in these parts, for this time of year, has been at its worse. The ferocity of the storms and the extreme rainfall, have been dangerous to those residing in the region. What has been most concerning this year however, is the unpredictability of these catastrophic, perilous storms, leaving no warning to those who will be impacted by their force.

From inside my room, I can hear Dad tearing up the TV room. Glass smashes against both the wooden and tiled floors with such force, it sends a spine-tingling jolt through me.

His frustrations are pouring out in a groaning roar. Chairs scrape violently across the floor with piercing screeches, followed by thuds as they come to an abrupt, heavy stop.

Then— silence.
Nothing.

It's probably only 30 seconds of absolute stillness, but I'm more afraid for Dad in that moment than I was during his entire rampage.
I wonder what he'll do next. If he's okay. How far he might go.

I hear his footsteps stomping past my door, fading into the distance. The front door flings open, then slams shut. Silence returns.

I force myself to take a slow, measured breath. As I exhale, his words echo through my mind: *It should have been you.*

It's like I'm frozen in place, trapped in a trance. I can't move. Only my chest moves— rising and falling, rising and falling, rising and falling.

As the wet season draws to a close and the dry season begins, the boab tree is transforming itself into its most iconic state. As a deciduous tree, they lose all of their leaves during the dry season. What will be left, are skeletal branches and its bulbous trunk that becomes accentuated by the loss of leaves. The bark is of grey, brown appearance and has a surprisingly smooth texture. This is a most amazing tree.

I step out of my bedroom. The house is eerily quiet. As I approach the doorway at the end of the hall, I squint hard, trying to make out the outlines of furniture thrown out of place.

I take a few slow, careful steps and immediately feel the crunch of shattered glass beneath the soles of my shoes.

My shin slams into something solid. I yelp and bend to rub it. As I do, I reach out and feel for the object responsible.

But it's not that I feel. It's a frame.

Not just any frame. *Their* wedding photo, the one taken at Knight's Park under the boab tree.

I know this wasn't what I banged into, but I can hardly believe Dad would throw it around like trash.

I thought he was only angry at *me.*

But maybe... he's just as mad at *her* too.

Still squatting, I feel around with my right hand.

There it is.

The leg of one of our dining chairs. No wonder my shin is throbbing. This thing is solid enough to leave a deep bruise.

I prop the chair upright, carefully place the frame on it, and push it out of the way.

I turn to leave the room, realising what a bad idea it was to come in here in the first place. Glass everywhere. Furniture tossed around. Too much risk.

As I pivot, my legs catch on something else. I lose balance. Arms flail.

I brace myself with my hands out, ready for the fall.

Impact.

Pain.

A fiery jolt races up my arms as sharp glass pierces my palms. I scream out. The sound slices through the empty house.

Slowly, I lift each hand and turn them toward my face. I'm looking straight at them.

But I see no red.

No blood.

Just rough outlines.

Not long ago, I could see colours— brilliant, dizzying colours. Now, there's nothing but shadow.

I rise unsteadily, careful not to use my hands. In the hallway, I start the agonising task of inspecting my wounds. I use my left fingers to gently probe my right hand.

I find the first shard.

Pinch it like tweezers. Count to three.

Then yank.

I repeat the process again and again, removing every fragment I can feel.

Eventually, all I feel is a wet, sticky mess of blood and flesh.

I can only *hope* I got everything.

There's no way I'm asking Dad for help. No chance I'm going to the local doctor.

Can you imagine?

"Hi Doctor, I'm Owen. Just moved here."

"How did you get glass in your hands?"

"Oh, well... my dad told me I should've died instead of my mum, and then *he*, not me, trashed the house."

Yeah. No thanks.

I know I need water. Cold water.

The safest option is my own bathroom.

I shuffle through the hall, taking tiny steps. I can't fall again.

I turn on the tap.

Let the cold water run over my torn-up hands.

The sting is unbearable. But I'm relieved to be out of that glass-filled, over-turned furniture war zone.

I wrap a towel around my hands, squeezing tightly, trying to stop the bleeding.

No idea if it's working.

Still clutching the towel, I stumble back to my bed and collapse onto it.

My mind is spinning.

Questions. Doubts. Emotions.

But mostly, just the same sentence on repeat.

It should have been you.

It should have been you.

It should have been you.

Boabs must survive in the harshest of climates. During the wet season, boab's store water in their trunks, allowing them to replenish during the dry season as well as somewhat protect them from the heat of bushfires. They are however susceptible, although resilient, to bush fires. If bark is burnt it peels off to reveal a fresh layer underneath. Such a wonderous ability to be able to endure a natural disaster, survive it, and come through on the other side, restored.

CHAPTER 17

IN MY HEAD

I drag my feet along the gravel road, not caring if I stub my toe or trip over some unseen object.

I'm too lost in my own head, replaying the argument with Dad over and over. I hear his words again, and they cut deeper than the glass shards did in my hands.

I re-enact the fight, creating different versions of the truth, anything to make me feel better. Or angrier. Or justified.

In one version, I storm back into the TV room, stand right in front of him, and scream as loudly as I can. My fists are clenched, eyes closed, and the screaming acts as a release like an eruption of emotion from deep within the pit of my stomach.

Dad begins crying, apologising, finally realising. But instead of relenting, I snarl at him, then maniacally start pushing over furniture, smashing glassware, destroying the room. Just like he did. As if it were me all along, not him.

I keep walking, pretending I have no destination. But my feet say otherwise. They've traced this path too many times since we moved to Wanooni.

I come to the main intersection and cross like I've done a heap of times before. The street is deserted. No cars, no people— just the wind rustling the leaves.

Normally, I'd use nature's sounds to tune into other subtle noises. Playing a kind of mindfulness game, I came up with since losing most of my sight. It helps calm me down. Helps stop the overthinking.

But not now. Not today.

I walk with even more purpose. It's not long before I'm standing in front of the boab.

I wait.

For her.

I need to talk.

I need answers.

I need someone to listen to me, like she used to.

Where is she?

She's always here.

It feels like I've been waiting for hours, though it's probably only a few minutes.

My thoughts race. My anger builds. I feel like I might explode if I don't let it out.

Where is she?

Why aren't you here?

I need...

She's gone.

She doesn't care.

If she did, she'd be here.

It's my fault. It's always my fault.

I scared her away last time.

I'm too difficult.

I do stupid things.

I stifle the tears bursting behind my eyes like a dam about to give way. My mouth is dry, throat clogged. My eyes wide open, held there by something invisible and unrelenting.

My breathing is sharp, erratic. Despite the pain, my hands clench into fists, stretching rigidly at my sides.

Then I snap.

I launch into a fit of punching and kicking. Each impact collides with the trunk of the boab— fast, but weakening with every blow.

"Hey! Stop that! You're gonna hurt yourself!" yells a man. His hands clasp my shoulders firmly and pull me back. "That's enough, mate."

His voice is kind but assertive.

In that moment, my body and mind return to me. My knuckles sting. My toes throb.

I can hardly believe what just happened. A total loss of control. It was like being in a trance, like someone else had the controller and were double-tapping the X and O. "Come with us. We'll take you home, hey?" says the man.

For the first time, I turn toward him. I notice another figure behind him, and flashing lights from a car nearby. "Oh."

"Don't worry, we'll take you home. You're new here, yeah? You Patrick's boy?"

"Yeah. Owen," I say, deflated.

"Well, Owen, I'm Rick. Most folks just call me Officer Rick."

We drive slowly through the main street. The air con is blasting and it's freezing in the car.

Goosebumps rise along my arms. I rub them to keep warm, although I'm not sure if it's from the air or the shivers still crawling up my spine from being in a too-familiar situation.

Finally, we pull up outside the house.

"Well, that answers that," says Officer Rick.

"I didn't ask a question," the other officer replies.

"Oh nah, I was talkin' to meself. Wondered if Pat'd be home. And sure enough, there he is."

"Am I in trouble?" I ask, the words falling out.

I hear the officer shift in his seat to face me.

"Nah, you're not in trouble. Well... not really. But we can't have ya goin' around beatin' up poor defenceless trees, can we?"

He sighs.

"Look, we just wanna make sure you and your dad are okay. Are ya?"

I don't know what to say. I lower my head and nod quickly.

"We know things weren't easy before you came to Wanooni. Heck, they're probably still a bit rough, yeah? If you ever want to chat, I'd be happy to listen."

"Thanks," I mumble, feeling for the door handle.

"Oh, I'll come 'round and let you out. We don't normally just let our passengers jump out by themselves," he chuckles.

We walk toward the house. One officer stays in the car, while Rick walks ridiculously close to me— his shoulder brushes mine.

Not sure if he thinks I'll bolt, or if he's trying to guide me.

"Hi Patrick, just making sure Owen got home safely," says Officer Rick.

"Well, thank you very much, Officer," Dad replies from the front porch.

"How 'bout you go inside, Owen, clean yourself up a bit, while I have a quick chat with, ya old man?"

Great. He's going to tell Dad what I did. My bruised knuckles will give it away anyway.

Why should I care? I mean, Dad destroyed the whole TV room.

I smirk at the thought: I should invite the officer in, tell him to sit there. Let him see it all for himself.

But I let the thought pass. I couldn't do that. Not to Dad.

No matter how angry I am. It'd be a low blow.

Even for me.

I walk up the stairs, past Dad, and head straight inside.

The cold water over my hands is like moisturiser on sunburn. Soothing.

I stand there, letting the water run, terrified of the idea that I might lose myself like that again.

Knock, knock.

Dad stands in the ensuite doorway.

"I'm really sorry for what I said, Owen. I didn't mean it. You just caught me... in a moment."

I don't care.

I push past him, ignoring his words.

"Owen?" he asks, waiting.

"Whatever. I'm tired. I'm going to bed," I say, dismissively.

I collapse onto my bed, facing the wall.

Dad leaves without another word.

I sigh loudly. For once, my mind is too exhausted to think.

And I'm glad for it.

I don't want to think about the last time I was in the back of a police car.

I don't want to think about how I completely lost myself tonight.

I don't want to think about his words.

CHAPTER 18
THE AFTER SHOCK

"What happened to your knuckles?" Jo asks in a concerned tone.

"None of your business," I reply.

"She was just asking," retorts Derek.

"Back off, nerd!" I snap, pushing my way through the classroom door. I head straight for the back of the room, just wanting to sink into my seat and let this day be over already.

"Good morning, Owen, Derek, Jo," says Mr. Peters in his usual cheerful tone.

Of all the classes, science is the absolute last place I want to be today. I just need to get through this one session, and then I have Ms. Donnington. I never thought I'd be happy for my one-on-one sessions with her, but right now, I just don't want to be around lots of people. Especially *these* people.

If Mr. Peters asks me just one question, I swear I will run out of here or completely lose it.

"Owen?" says Mr. Peters.

"Huh?" I reply, caught off guard.

"I'm doing the roll call, Owen. Just a 'yes' will suffice."

The class lets out a laugh, which both angers and embarrasses me.

I hate science.

I hate this school.

I wish we never moved here.

"Okay class," says Mr. Peters, "I thought it might be fun to pause our work on black holes, at least until next week, and instead today... conduct some experiments."

The class cheers, and even I find myself with a half-smile. It's a smile of relief, I think. Not having to concentrate or worry about being called upon to answer some stupid question.

"So, can everyone get into groups of three while I set up a few things?"

Oh, great, I think to myself. I stay in my seat, hoping I don't have to be in a group. Maybe I could just do it with Mr. Peters or even one other random person.

Or better yet, maybe he'll think I'm a hazard and tell me I can sit this one out.

"How's it looking? Is everyone in a three? Jo and Derek, who's your third?"

"Can't we just work as a two?" asks Jo.

"Hmm, you might... oh hang on, Owen. What group are you in?" Mr. Peters asks.

You've got to be kidding me. Of all the groups, I definitely don't want to be with *them*. He better not—

"I can just—" I begin.

"Yes, perfect. You can join Jo and Derek to make a three," he interrupts.

I roll my eyes and let out an audible groan.

"Is there a problem, Owen?" Mr. Peters asks.

"You mean besides being grouped with the nerds? No, everything is *amazing*," I say scathingly, flashing a big fake smile as the rest of the class laughs.

"Owen, we don't name-call in this class. And we also don't

judge people before getting to know them."

Is he for real? My anger boils over.

"Everyone judges *me*, what's the difference? Calling them nerds is one of the nicest things I could've said. I could've called them teacher's pets."

The class laughs again, fuelling me further.

"Or boring. Or midgets. Well, at least the last one for Derek," I chuckle.

"That's enough, Owen. I think you can sit out of the experiments today. Jo and Derek shouldn't have to put up with that."

I take a few deep breaths, trying to calm myself.

"Fantastic!" I say sarcastically.

"I'll give you some worksheets to do instead. Oh, um..." His voice trails off, realising that worksheets won't really work in my case.

I smirk. He knows I've played this to my advantage.

"I'll see if Ms. Donnington can come early and help out," he says.

My smirk widens into a relieved grin. I can finally get out of here.

"Okay, everyone else, let me explain each of the experiments, and then we can start the rotation."

My smile fades as I'm left alone with my thoughts. Mr. Peters and the drone of my classmates become a background hum.

It was never a good idea to come to school today. I don't know why I did. After yesterday. After last night. I could've easily convinced Dad to let me stay home.

But I think the problem is, that would've meant being *stuck* at home. With *him*.

As much as I didn't want to go to school, I wanted to be home even less.

If I hadn't come today, there'd just be pressure to come the next day, then the next. Then Lina would be on my back too.

I can't handle another person interfering right now.

I really wish everyone would just leave me alone.

"Ahh, Ms. Donnington, thanks for coming so quickly," says Mr. Peters.

"No worries. Shall we have a chat first?" I hear Ms. Donnington say.

"Okay class, you have three more minutes at your current station. You should be writing down your findings by now."

Mr. Peters and Ms. Donnington are outside having a chat. By now, they've figured out that my hearing is pretty good, so if they want to talk about me, they have to be far enough away.

I can guess what they're saying, though. Hopefully, they agree I'm not ready for mainstream science and Ms. Donnington can take me for that too.

They walk back in, and Ms. Donnington heads straight for me at the back of the room.

"Had a tough morning?" she asks.

"Yeah," I reply with a sigh.

"Do you want to come with me, or stay and do some Science worksheets?" she teases.

"Are you *for real*?" I ask, grinning.

"Yes, I'm for real. Come on then, before I change my mind."

I can hardly believe it. I shove my things into my bag as fast as I can.

Maybe I misjudged Ms. Donnington. She knew, without me saying a word, exactly what I wanted— what I *needed*: to be out of this room.

She places my hand gently on her shoulder, and I walk behind her as she guides me easily out of the noisy classroom.

As we walk along the corridor, she doesn't once mention

how I behaved. We reach the library, and instead of sitting beside me, I feel sheets of paper fall lightly onto the backs of my hands.

"I'm just helping the librarian this session," she says. "If you want to practise your braille, there are some alphabet sheets in front of you. Otherwise, if you just want to chill for the next ten minutes, that's okay too. Unless..." she pauses, "do you want to use this time to talk to me about something?"

The question catches me off guard. My first instinct is to shake my head.

"I thought that might be the case. I'm just in the next room if you need me. We'll start our session in about ten minutes," she says.

"Okay," I manage.

CHAPTER 19
LIFE SUPPORT

I don't remember lights ever being this bright. There must be hundreds of them in this tiny room, all turned up to their most luminous setting. My eyes squint, trying to shield themselves from their boldness.

I can see a figure lying in the bed, arms by their side, the bed slightly angled upright. Motionless.

The heart monitor emits a high-pitched beep in a steady rhythm. Like a drumbeat keeping time: BEEP, pause, BEEP, pause, BEEP.

The pauses are just long enough to make you hold your breath, anxiously waiting... hoping, for the next sound.

For every three beeps of the monitor, the ventilator forces air into the lungs. It lets out a sound like a tire being deflated, overpowering the beeps.

BEEP, pause, BEEP, pause, BEEP, COOOSSSHHHH!

BEEP, pause, BEEP, pause, BEEP, COOOSSSHHHH!

BEEP, pause, BEEP, pause, BEEP, COOOSSSHHHH!

My body feels weak.

I'm tired, sore, and in a constant dazed state. But it's sadness that conquers everything.

My throat is dry and stinging. My eyes are swollen with tears.

My eyebrows are pulled up and together, my eyelids heavy.

My lips droop downward.

My chest feels like it's bound by rope, being pulled tighter and tighter.

Each limb weighs a tonne, like the mass of a cruise ship, and I can hardly move at all.

That's the control sadness has over me. It consumes me entirely.

Sadness for the situation.

Sadness for us.

Sadness for me.

There was Dad, standing beside me, his hand on my shoulder, muttering words I couldn't understand.

He, too, was overcome with grief. I couldn't see him clearly, but I didn't have to. His shaky, softened voice betrayed his tear-streaked cheeks and hunched posture.

His words repeated over and over, but still, I couldn't make sense of them.

"Dad? What are you saying? Dad? I can't hear you! Dad? Tell me what's happening! Dad? What happened? DAD!!!"

"Owen, it's okay. I'm here. It's okay, Owen. I'm sorry. I never meant it. I never meant any of it. I'm sorry. Owen? Please wake up. You're having a bad dream. A nightmare. Owen? It's okay. I'm here. Owen?"

I jolt upright, startled, ripped awake from it.

The nightmare.

The reality.

My breathing is laboured and heavy. I take a moment to calm it and adjust to what's real. I'm in this bed, in this house in Wanooni. Back in the present.

But I feel five years old again, with Dad sitting at the edge of my bed, hugging me, telling me everything is okay.

My pyjamas are soaked with sweat. My eyes are puffy and wet.

I used to have nightmares all the time when I was little.

Usually about dinosaurs chasing me or getting stuck in quicksand.

Dad would come into my room, bring me warm milk, and cuddle me with my teddy, Angus. He'd make Angus talk in a silly voice, promising to guard me all night and protect me from anything.

After enough convincing, and dragging it out so Dad would stay, I'd go back to sleep, feeling safe.

Back then, I was sure Angus would protect me from everything.

I feel Dad's hand gently rubbing my shoulders.

"You okay now, mate?" he asks softly.

I nod, unable to speak, the memory of my nightmare still vivid in my mind.

"I really am sorry for what I said yesterday," he says.

"I know," I manage to whisper through my tight throat.

"But I want you to really know. I don't blame you. For any of it.

I miss her. Your mum. I've just been so angry, and I shouldn't have taken it out on you.

I'm your dad. I want you to be able to talk to me. I want to listen, to be there for you.

And I know I haven't been. You've been through so much—

more than any twelve-year-old should.

I'm sorry. I want to do better. I *will* do better."

"I know. I really know," I say.

There's silence, but not the kind that's filled the house for months.

This silence feels peaceful. For the first time, in a long time.

I lay back down, still exhausted and ready to sleep again.

"Do you need a warm milk and perhaps Angus to help you fall asleep?" Dad asks playfully.

"Haha, no, I'm not a little kid anymore," I reply.

"What are you talking about? You don't have to be little to love Angus. I love Angus, and I'm a grown man. Where is he, by the way?"

"He's in my cupboard. I'll always like Angus... but I'm old enough to know he can't actually protect me from nightmares."

Dad opens the cupboard.

"You've hurt Angus's feelings," he says. "Maybe he needs to stay in my room now. Protect me. Hmm... actually, maybe from tomorrow. I'm pretty wrecked myself, and by the looks of this cupboard, he won't be easy to find."

A smile flashes across my face as I close my eyes and

allow my body to finally relax.

"Good night, Dad."

"Night, Owen."

CHAPTER 20

TRUTH IS IN REALITY

"Where were you? I needed you, and you weren't here," I say, crouching down in front of the now very familiar boab tree. I start using some of my breathing techniques to calm myself, and even the thought of Dad, and last night's conversation, brings a small sense of relief.

I don't want the shopkeeper coming out, or worse, getting picked up by Officer Rick again.

I have so many questions I need her to answer. My insides burn and ache, the nausea rising up my oesophagus and pausing at its peak— never quite letting go, never quite letting me be. I don't know what's worse: actually vomiting, or the constant feeling of needing to.

"Owen, are you okay?" asks Sonia.

I stand up and spin around so quickly I nearly lose my balance, saved only by my outstretched arms.

"Where have you been?" I demand, trying to focus on her as much as possible so she doesn't disappear again.

"Owen. You know the answer to that," she says, her voice carrying an unfamiliar sadness.

"No, I don't! I came here the other day looking for you, and you weren't here. And the two times before that, I was talking to you, and you just... left. I don't know where you went. I don't understand– you're always here," I say, mournfully, tears filling my eyes.

"Owen. Do you know where the name Sonia comes from?" she asks.

"What? What are you talking about?" I ask, confused.

"Sonia comes from *Adansonia*--- the genus made up of eight species of deciduous trees. One of which is the baobab," she says.

"What does that even mean?" I cry.

"It's why I chose that name, Owen. So, you'd know it

was me. So, you'd know... I'm not..."

My eyes, already brimming with tears, begin to betray me again. Semi-circles of colour flash across my vision. I see her— really see her— for the first time. Not clearly, but through fractured, coloured diamond-shapes trying to fit together, trying to show me the truth.

It's Sonia. Except... she isn't Sonia. I know exactly who she is.

I suppose I've always known. She was the only one who ever really listened.

It's her.

I've wanted to have her with me again. That's why I've always come here. To this spot. To this tree.

I missed her. So much that I...

...I made her real again.

She was never really here, because—

* * *

"That's not how it works Owen and you know it," smirks Mum as she raises from her slumped position. *"If you want the front seat, you have to play for it,"* she declares.

"Aren't I getting too old for playing these kid games?" I ask, pretending they annoy me.

"You'll always be my kid," she says. "And besides, you want to sit in the front seat, don't you?"

I sigh, pretending to be bored. "Yeah."

Mum nods to herself. "Well, I'm going to make you earn it for as long as I can get away with it."

"Okay, let's play then," I say still acting like I don't care.

"Good! Here's your riddle: what kind of balls don't bounce?" Mum asks gleefully, pointing to her watch.

"I know this... I get one minute. I should know this. Urgh! What balls don't bounce? Oh— eyeballs! It's eyeballs!" I shout, excited.

Dad's head swivels around, scanning the café nervously, then sends me a look that clearly says: *Be quiet.* Meanwhile, Mum is grinning from ear to ear, trying to stifle a laugh.

"Yes, eyeballs are correct," she finally says.

"Your turn. I read this one the other day— it's super tricky. You'll never get it."

"Yeah, yeah, get on with it."

"Okay, your riddle is: *The bigger I become, the less you see. What is it?*" I ask.

"The bigger I become, the less you see?" Mum repeats.

I point to her watch and she nods knowingly.

"Well, this is tricky. I get three guesses though, remember?" she says.

"Yep!" I reply, flashing a wide grin.

"Yes, I know, I know. I still have forty-eight seconds. Now... the bigger it gets, the less you see. Arghhhh, I don't know. I can only think of actual things, which make no sense. What's something that's not a thing?" Mum mutters to herself.

I point to her watch again, smug. She looks genuinely stumped. Her expression says it all, defeat and frustration, as she checks the time.

"Seven seconds," I tease.

"Four, three, two, one... time's up. I win," I announce with a chuckle.

"Well, what is it? What can't you see, the bigger it becomes?" she asks, annoyed.

"No, no— it's *the bigger I become, the less YOU see,*" I say, emphasising *you.*

"Huh?" says Mum, utterly confused.

"Darkness," I say proudly.

"What? How does darkness become bigger? That doesn't make any sense."

"Yes, it makes perfect sense. Those are the rules, let's

not change them now. I believe I get to ride shotgun on the way home?" I ask with a laugh.

I sat in the front seat, feeling the happiest I had felt all week. I was in a good mood, one of my favourite songs was on the radio, and for once, Dad had let me turn the volume up a few notches. Even the dark clouds looming low in the sky, threatening to enclose around us, couldn't dampen my spirits.

"I'm surprised they haven't closed this highway yet," says Dad.

"Yeah, give it a few more days. They'll have to. I'm glad they haven't yet though. It's a lot quicker. We'll be home in no time," Mum replies from the seat behind me.

No sooner had she spoken than the rain poured down, hammering the car. Dad cranked the windscreen wipers to their fastest setting— the one Mum calls 'crazy-mode.'

I could see Dad leaning forward and squinting, trying to make out the road ahead.

"Owen, turn down the music— I need to concentrate," Dad says abruptly.

"Okay, okay, no need to shout," I say, speaking loud enough to be heard over the storm.

"Owen, the music!"

"Relax, would ya? I'm turning it—"

Then I saw them.

Two bright lights, glaring ahead, coming at us faster than my brain could process.

"Dad, look ou—!"

He already knew.

He was yanking the steering wheel hard to the right, trying to avoid a head-on collision. The other vehicle was on the wrong side of the road— directly in front of us, closing in fast.

We veered sharply, and I felt our car start to slide. The oncoming vehicle's headlights passed by the passenger side, so close, but just as I thought we'd made it, there was a jolt.

Their left front bumper clipped the back of our car, just enough to send us spinning.

Dad wrestled with the steering wheel, trying to correct the skid, but it wouldn't move. It was jammed or useless now.

We looked at each other.

Dad's eyes wide with fear. I'd never seen him like that.

Then, through the torrential rain, I spotted it: a large boab tree on the side of the road.

I wasn't even sure if it was real. Everything felt surreal—like slow motion and the tree appeared to glow.

It was as if I could trace a perfect, invisible line from our spinning car straight to the tree. Just under a hundred metres to go.

We were still rotating. But our path was locked in.

The only question left in my mind was this:

What part of the car would hit first?

The force of impact would be massive.

And surely... fatal.

BANG!

The sound was the loudest, most horrifying noise I have ever heard. The car is pulverised by the huge base of the boab.

The back passenger car door buckle and collapse under the might of it.

The impact fatal. Later the doctors would remark in astonishment at the severity of the accident's impact on the back passenger door wasn't what actually killed her, but the complications that followed.

Fragments shot through the air, piercing anything in its path. The window next to me shatters fiercely into thousands of pieces, some ricocheting off my body while others lodge deep inside my flesh.

My forehead smashes the door frame, knocking me unconscious. The next thing I remember, I am surrounded by dark figures. There are sirens, and the only thing drowning it out is the sound of a shrieking and blood-curdling cry. I soon realise that the cry is coming from me.

* * *

I'm holding Mum's hand as she lies motionless in the hospital bed. The doctor is talking to Dad, but they might as well be speaking another language. I can't understand a word they're saying.

Mum's been on life support since the accident a few months ago. We've both been in the hospital all this time, but I haven't been able to visit her much.

"Owen, do you understand?" Dad asks.

"What?" I mutter.

"Do you understand what the doctor is saying, Owen?"

"No," I reply simply.

"Your Mum has shown no signs of improvement since the accident. She is only alive because the machine..." Dad's voice trails off, not wanting to finish the sentence. I try to grasp what he is saying.

And then I know.

"She going to die, isn't she?" I ask abruptly.

"Yeah," Dad says despondently.

* * *

I'm standing by the boab tree out front of the shop, tears flowing freely down my cheeks as sound memories take over me.

The day we took her off life support.

Hearing her last breath.

The sound of the machine flat-lining.

The day of her funeral.

Their words on repeat: *we're sorry for your loss, we're sorry for your loss, we're sorry for your loss.*

The emptiness of the house once everyone had left. I reach out, hoping she'll be there– to hug me, to tell me everything is going to be okay.

But she doesn't... because... she's not here.

She's never been here.

She's gone.

Her.

My mum.

"Owen? It's me. You're going to be okay, mate. Let's get you home to ya ole man," says Officer Rick.

CHAPTER 21

THE KNOWING

"Hi Patrick, good to see ya," says Officer Rick.

"Hi Rick. I am beginning to think the police around here have nothing better to do than bring my son home," laughs Dad, placing a hand on my shoulder and guiding me inside.

"Hahaha, don't tell anyone, will ya," jokes Officer Rick.

I make my way down the hallway as Dad and Officer Rick continue exchanging jokes.

I stop at the entrance to the kitchen and TV room,

unsure where to place myself. I'd like to say I'm in shock after what just happened at the boab, but... I'm not. The thing is, I always knew— just like she said I did.

Sonia was never real. I wanted her to be, because if she was, it would mean Mum was still here. But I know she's not. I was there in the car when we crashed into the boab— when it violently demolished the back passenger side of the car, right where Mum was sitting.

I was there in the hospital room when she was on life support. I was there, holding her hand, when they turned it off.

Sonia was a figment of my imagination. She was my mum—someone who listened to me, who made the relationship between Dad and me manageable. Someone who put up with me but never let me get away with anything.

My thoughts are interrupted by the lowered voices coming from out front. I tilt my head and can just make out their words.

"I found him outside the corner store again."

"Was he punching and kicking the tree again?"

"Nah, worse."

"Worse? How can it be worse? I thought we made some progress— things seemed good after..."

"Pat, I found him cryin'. It looked like he was just staring up at that big ole boab and bawlin' his eyes out. What is it about him and that tree?"

"Oh, I see. Yeah, that's a bit of a story, that one, Rick. And I'm not sure I'm up to telling it tonight."

"Ain't none of my business. Look, he'll be right, mate. I just can't have him trashin' anything, but I'm always happy to bring him home. It's the least I can do."

I move deeper into the kitchen, then into the TV room. I've heard enough. I walk cautiously across the room, imagining the absolute mess it must've been earlier. But it's just in my head— there's no sign of upturned furniture or shattered glass. Everything is back in place.

I know I can take a direct path to the couch without bumping into anything, though the thought makes me instinctively bend down and rub the bruised shin that smacked into the dining chair.

I hear Dad say goodbye to Rick, followed by the front door closing. I make my way to the couch and sit down, almost melting into its softness as I wait for Dad. He'll want to talk.

"Officer Rick is a very nice man, isn't he?" Dad offers as he enters the room.

"Yeah," I reply.

"What's going on, Owen? I thought we were getting somewhere after last night."

I know I just need to be honest, tell him how I've been feeling and what I think I've been seeing. It all just spills out.

"I miss her so much. We used to talk... a lot."

"I can't imagine what it feels like to lose your mum. I'm sorry it happened to you, Owen. Can you talk to me? I know it won't be the same, but I can listen."

"You don't listen to me, Dad. That's the problem!" I shout, frustrated.

"I know. I need to get better. All I can say is that I promise I'll try. How about you try me now? Tell me something—about school, or your friends, or how you've been feeling. Anything."

I take a deep breath. In my mind, I question whether I should even try. I know what I want to talk about, but I keep thinking about how the last conversation went. What would make this time any different?

Then I remember what Sonia said: *You'll never know if you don't even try.*

"I want to play Goalball. It's a sport."

I pause, waiting for him to interrupt me. To say no. But

he doesn't.

So, I continue, "You wear these eye covers to play so no one can see anything, and there's a ball with bells in it. You have to score by throwing the ball into the goals."

"Oh! That's what you were trying to tell me the other day, wasn't it? But I wasn't listening."

I feel guilty for how I've been treating him. He's only been doing what he thought was best for me.

"It's okay. I haven't been very... nice to you. I've been a bit of a brat," I admit, knowing that's the kindest way to put it.

He rests a hand on my shoulder. "Well, let's both promise to do better. We need to tell each other what we want, and how we feel, while the other person listens. Deal?"

I smile and nod. For the first time, I know things can get better— if I give it a chance.

"I know in the past I put my work first, but I've already told them that I can't do that anymore. I need to spend more time with you. It's important. So, looks like I'll be watching a few games of Goalball, hey?" Dad laughs.

My smile fades as I remember what happened in science class.

"I don't know... The people who invited me to play, I

was really mean to them. They probably don't want me there anymore."

"I'm sure that's not true. Just talk to them. Kids are pretty good at forgiving," he says knowingly.

Just then, a flash of light stuns me. I jerk back on the couch as if to brace myself. I blink several times and then see the colour blue— a dark blue, rectangular shape.

It's the TV.

"Owen, what's wrong?" Dad asks.

My mouth opens in excitement. I blink again, turning my head, and I see dark red. I can't make out what it is, but I smile, thrilled by the sight of another colour. I look in the direction of my dad, who's a mix of dark red, blue, and black.

"Owen?" he asks more urgently this time, trying to understand what's happening.

"Sorry— but I'm okay. More than okay, actually," I say, trying to calm him while still captivated by what I'm seeing.

I stand up to get a better view and tell him, "I can see... well, colours. I can see colours. Blue, red, and now yellow. I saw them the other day too, and earlier. I think I'm starting to get my sight back."

I let out a small giggle. I feel like a kid who's just been

told they're going to Disneyland. It's everything I've ever wanted.

"Really? So, you can see the colour of the shirt I'm wearing?"

"Nah, haha. I'm just seeing colours. Like when I look at you, I see a lot of different colours that don't really make colour sense. Haha, I don't know if I'm making any sense."

"It's a start, Owen. You're seeing something you weren't before. I don't want you to get your hopes up just yet, though. We'll need to book in with Dr. Simmons and see what he has to say."

I know he's right. I shouldn't get my hopes up.

But this is the third time in two days that I've seen colour.

How can this be anything but good news?

Everything has been so bad; maybe this is the start of everything good.

I'm going to fix things with Jo and Derek.

Well, I'm going to try.

Because *you'll never know if you don't even try.*

CHAPTER 22

SHEDDING MY SKIN

There they are. It's gotta be them. Who else would be waiting outside class ten minutes before it even starts?

Even though I'm back to my dark, shadowy vision, I've come to recognise their outlines. The colours I saw yesterday lasted longer than they did the first few times, but disappointingly, the darkness still came back.

I knock the thought out of my head. I have a job to do, and it's not one I'm looking forward to.

"Hey, Jo. Derek!" I call out to get their attention,

knowing they'll be doing everything they can to avoid me today. Maybe for the rest of my life here. I don't blame them.

"What do you want?" snaps Derek.

"I know. I was an idiot," I say.

"An idiot? You were more than just an idiot," Jo adds.

"I know. I'm sorry. I was frustrated, and there's been a lot going on and..."

"Yeah, but what you said in science yesterday— that wasn't cool. Like, really not cool," says Jo.

I know I'm just giving them excuses. I don't really know what to say to make it okay. I just know I want it to be. But before I can say anything else, Derek interrupts.

"Come on, Jo. We've got English."

I'm left standing there alone as their shadows move further and further away from me.

How could I think that just saying sorry would make it all okay?

I want to get out of here, skip school, but I'm done with that. I can't keep running every time things get tough. I promised Dad I'd do better. Try harder.

There's nothing I can do right now to fix things with Jo and Derek, so I begin to make my way to the library where

Ms. Donnington will be waiting for our English session.

"Hi, Owen. Head straight in. I won't be a sec," says Ms. Donnington as I enter the library.

I do as she says and sit down in the same chair I've used for every one-on-one session so far.

Come to think of it, I actually think Ms. Donnington's pretty cool. Well, at least after that first session where she tried to get me to listen to braille on boabs. For a teacher, she's alright.

I mean, imagine if someone like Lina was my teacher. I reckon she would've been on my case all the time, and Dad would've known about the time I stormed off. I couldn't have dealt with that.

"Sorry about that, Owen. I've got everything we need now. It's just been a bit of a morning, so I didn't get the time," says Ms. Donnington as she walks in.

"Yeah," I reply, completely understanding.

I'm immediately distracted by my own thoughts, thinking about this morning and how badly my apology went with Jo and Derek.

She must notice me drifting. "Is everything okay, Owen? You know you can talk to me if you need to."

"Yeah, it's fine. What are we doing today?" I ask, trying

to change the subject quickly.

I know I *can* talk to her, but I'm actually okay. The best I've been in a while, really. All I've been doing lately is talking. Today, I just want to get through school and *not* think about all that stuff.

Not Dad. Not Mum.
And definitely not Jo and Derek.

"Okay, well then let's make a start, shall we? How do you feel about snakes?"

The question throws me off a bit, but I'm happy she's changing the topic.

"Yeah, I reckon they're pretty cool."

"Would you ever have one as a pet?"

"A snake? That'd be awesome, but Dad would never let me."

I remember asking for a pet mouse when I was younger and getting a definite no. I wouldn't even bother asking for a snake.

"I think that's fair enough. Anyway, the reason I asked is because today I've got a couple of paragraphs in braille about snakes shedding their skin. I thought I could read it first while you trace it with your hands. Then I'll ask you a few questions about it, and after that, you can have a go at reading it yourself. Sound good?"

She's always so excited about our lessons, it's hard to match that energy, but I try.

"Yeah, awesome!"

How Snakes Shed their Skin

Snakes are remarkable creatures with the ability to shed their own skin. Some species do this once a month, while others may only do it a few times a year. The process begins when a new layer of skin forms beneath the old one. Shedding starts near their mouth and works its way down their body.

Why Snakes Shed their Skin?

There are two main reasons why snakes shed their skin: Their skin does not grow, so when a snake's body grows, its skin becomes stretched.

Snakes collect dirt, bacteria, and harmful parasites on their skin. Shedding gives them the chance to get rid of all of it.

"Okay, Owen, that'll be enough of the text. Let's do some questions. How often do snakes shed their skin?" asks Ms. Donnington.

"It depends on the type of snake. Some do it once a month, others a few times a year," I answer.

These questions are easy, I think to myself. But I know this isn't really about the answers, it's about how well I can read braille.

"That's good. Okay, just one more. In your opinion, what's the most interesting thing about snakes shedding their skin?"

I think about it for a while, even though I already know my answer. I was thinking about it the whole time she read the passage.

I get it. I really do. I understand why a snake needs to shed its skin.

In a weird way, I feel like I'm a snake— starting to shed my own skin.

I've had a buildup of all these things I couldn't let go of. They had a hold over me. And the more they built up, the more I couldn't handle it.

So, I'm shedding.

I'm getting rid of all the filth.

I'm getting a fresh, new skin.

A second chance.

She didn't get one— so that I could.

CHAPTER 23

COACH CARDIFF

I'm glad I remembered to wear my sunglasses today. Just like last time, the brightness inside is glaring and unbearable. Back then, I was outside, but now, from inside the court, the sunlight blazes through the glass windows just as much— maybe even worse.

I really don't know what I'm doing here. It's Thursday, and it's been days since Jo and Derek have spoken to me; since I tried to apologise to them about what happened in science class.

I want to play Goalball. It'd be so cool if I was on their

team. But maybe I'm too late. They only need three players, and they were just short one. They probably don't need me anymore.

I turn to walk out when a man's voice stops me: "Hello there, are you here for Goalball practice?"

"Umm, I don't know," I reply honestly.

"My name's Mike; everyone calls me Coach Cardiff. What's your name, kid?"

"I'm Owen," I say, remembering that it was Coach Cardiff's voice I heard explaining the rules when I came here last week.

"Oh, you're Jo's friend, right? She'll be so happy you made it to practice. And Derek, too. They said you'd be a great centre player."

I feel relieved they still need a teammate, and a centre player sounds important. But I'm worried Coach Cardiff has the old news. The updated news is that Jo and Derek want nothing to do with me. I'd be the last person they'd want on their team.

"Owen! You came!" Jo's familiar voice yells from behind me. Before I can turn around, I feel her hands on my shoulders pulling me in for a hug. I can't help but smile.

I start to say, "Look, I'm sorry about—"

"Yes! Now you can play centre for our team," Derek interrupts excitedly.

"It's okay. We forgive you, and you're here now," Jo adds.

"Cool. I don't know what centre is, but it sounds good," I say.

"All right, kids, let's get everyone sitting on the court," says Coach Cardiff.

I'm so excited to try out Goalball and finally play a team sport again. I put my hand on Derek's shoulder, letting him guide me to where we sit on the court. It's just another way to show I'm sorry for what I said in science last week.

"Okay everyone, let's get started with practice today. First, this is Owen; he'll be playing on Jo and Derek's team this season. Please make him feel welcome. Now, last week we talked about how you can shoot. Who can remind us of the rules?"

For the next ten minutes, Coach Cardiff bombards us with the rules of Goalball. He explains how the ball must be rolled or bowled to shoot, and any throws that don't touch the floor before the overthrow line result in a penalty. I don't exactly know what that means yet or where the overthrow line is, but I'm sure I'll work it out when I start playing.

Then he describes the court: nine metres wide by eighteen metres long, with duct tape marking the team areas where players must stay. Players can feel the tape with their hands, which helps them stay within bounds, he says.

More rules pour out of him like he's played the sport for years and could recite them in his sleep. He drones on:

12-minute halves.

After receiving control of the ball, your team has 10 seconds to throw it back at the opposing team's goal.

Every player must wear eye shades.

The referee must call 'play' to begin or restart the game.

It makes me wonder if Coach Cardiff actually did play Goalball, and maybe if he's partially blind like me.

Back in the hospital after the accident, there were other kids doing exercises to get better, but none had eye injuries. And despite Wanooni District High School specialising in vision impairment, I haven't met any kids like me. I thought before I got here there'd be a class full of blind kids that Ms. Donnington would teach. Except it's only ever been me.

For the first time, I realise this is something I've wanted— to meet someone going through what I am. I know lots of people have helped me, but I've felt so alone, like no one really understands.

Is that why I wanted to play Goalball? If anywhere would have someone with a visual impairment, it'd be here. I always thought it'd be another player, another kid, but maybe it's Coach Cardiff.

"Okay, let's go— get into your teams," Coach Cardiff interrupts my thoughts.

"Owen, go with Derek to our area; I'll get the eye shades," Jo instructs.

Derek guides me to our spot and tells me to bend down, still facing the same way, and feel the duct tape on the floor. I trace it with my fingertips along a straight line. It marks the edge of our area and the position I need to be in as centre player. I hear Jo's footsteps hurrying back excitedly and then feel what I think are the eye shades placed in my hand.

"Want me to put it on for you?" Jo asks.

"I need to put my sunglasses somewhere, but I can put this on," I say, adjusting the eye shade in my hand.

I feel my sunglasses being slid off my face, which I wasn't ready for, and my eyes squint at the sudden light seeping in.

"I'll give these to Coach Cardiff," Derek says, probably

talking about my sunglasses.

I'm relieved when I put on the eye shade. It instantly blocks out the glaring light. Any longer in that brightness and I think I would've gotten a headache.

Suddenly, I hear bells. They're getting louder, like they're coming right toward me.

Thud! The ball hits my upper thigh and stuns me.

"Great block, Owen!" yells Coach Cardiff.

I'm not sure if he's joking, but it doesn't bother me, I smile at the comment.

During practice, I'm the happiest I've been in a long time, laughing at my second-rate efforts to block shots and shoot at the goal. Coach tells us how far away we are from blocking and where our shots go, helping us adjust next time. I guess he can see just fine.

Jo, Derek, and I laugh every time we mess up. I think it's because this seemingly simple sport is actually really hard. It's definitely harder than I thought, and it's physical too, with its fast pace and diving either side on the hard floor. Coach keeps telling us to stop giggling so we can hear the ball better, and then maybe block shots more effectively.

Before I know it, Phooweet!

"Well done, everyone! That was a great practice

session. We've only got two more before games start, so make a real effort to get to them so we're well-prepared. Okay, please pack away the gear, and then you may go," Coach Cardiff instructs.

"That was so much fun," I say to Jo and Derek.

"You're pretty good at it too," Coach Cardiff says, handing me back my sunglasses.

I'm caught off guard by his presence and desperately want to ask if anyone who plays here is visually impaired.

But Jo interrupts, "Yeah, but he has a big advantage over us."

"Nah, you get to see the court. He never does," replies Coach Cardiff.

I take my chance. "Is anyone else here visually impaired, or is it just me?"

"Just you at the moment. There hasn't been anyone since Jordy, who moved out of Wanooni a couple of years back."

I kind of knew that was the truth all along, but I'm disappointed all the same.

"But you know," Coach Cardiff continues, "when I was twenty-three through twenty-seven, I had a vision impairment."

"Really?" I say, probably with too much excitement.

"Yeah, long story. I had cancer that messed with my vision. My eyes strained to compensate, but the only good it did was give me nasty headaches. In the end, I had to wear something like these eye shades, which made me completely blind for a few years. For someone who loved sport, it was torture. Well, at least until I found Goalball. Anyway, you three don't want to hear all of this. Go on, get out of here."

As we walk out of the rec centre, the relief I feel from Coach Cardiff's story is unexpected. It's like a weight was lifted from my chest, a weight that was crushing me, and now I can finally breathe. Someone just like me. Someone who experienced what I'm experiencing now. Someone who isn't blind anymore.

If my hope was a battery on charge, it went from empty to more than half full in an instant, with the final notch flashing, ready to turn solid.

"Hey Owen, will you ever see again? Like, properly?" Jo asks timidly.

"Yeah. Actually, just this week, I started seeing colours. So, I think I'm starting to get my vision back," I say with newfound confidence.

"That's awesome, Owen!" both Derek and Jo chorus.

I hear my dad's voice calling from the carpark.

"That's my dad. I have to go. Will I see you at school tomorrow?" I ask, uncertain if they're really my friends or if this is all just an act because they need me for Goalball.

"Yeah, we have Science first up. Let's meet out front before the bell. We can go together," Jo says.

CHAPTER 24

GOALBALL TOURNAMENT

One year later...

"Shhh, please. A reminder to the crowd *again* that Goalball is a silent spectator sport. Please, no cheering or clapping," says the referee.

I know this is aimed at my dad, and it just makes me laugh that he still hasn't worked it out, despite how many times I've told him. I turn my head toward the area in the crowd where I know he is and exaggerate a disapproving nod, in a mocking, playful kind of way.

"Derek, we need to keep it tight; there can't be long left. And Owen, if you can score one of your curve ball goals before time's up, that would be amazing," says Jo.

"*So* demanding," I reply cheekily, using the back of my hand to wipe the sweat from my hairline.

"Well, if we're going to win this game– and the tournament– a draw is not going to cut it," says Jo.

"Noted," I reply.

It's our final game of the season, and a win is the only option in my mind. I'm more determined than ever because it means so much after everything.

Phooweet.

"Owen, they've turned it over– the ball is yours, mate," instructs Coach Cardiff.

I hear the bell inside the ball jingle as it rolls slowly toward me. It's eerily quiet now; the only sound is the low hum of the distant pool motor outside the rec centre.

The ball reaches my hand with a soft slap. I grasp it firmly and focus on my breathing to steady myself. I know I've only got ten seconds to shoot once the ref calls play, but I plan to use every single one.

I want to take it all in.

Remember this moment.

As the ref yells **"Play!"** to resume the game, it's like he's switched on a movie theatre inside my head under the eye shades. The seconds tick down as memories from the past year flash before me...

Ten...

BANG!

In a strange, out-of-body way, I watch our car crash from above— like I'm hovering in a helicopter. But I know it's not someone else.

I know this happened to me.

It's our car.

That boab tree.

My mum.

My dad.

Me.

Nine...

BEEP. Pause. BEEP. Pause. BEEP. COOSSSHHHH.

I see myself at the hospital, sitting beside Mum, holding her hand. Dad's hand rests on my shoulder. He tells me the injuries were too much. Only the machines are keeping her alive.

We know we have to let her go.

Eight...

Such a strange place for a boab.

Such a strange place for a boab.

Such a strange place for a boab.

The thought echoes in my head as my forehead presses against the car window. I can almost feel the coolness if it wasn't for this searing heat.

I watch the outline of a boab tree in the middle of town.

Seven...

"You don't listen to me!" I hear myself shout.

"She wasn't supposed to be sitting there... you were!"

I stumble, trying to get away, but my legs fail. I grip the doorframe before sliding down.

I can see the exact moment my eyes see colour again for the first time. My head turning every which way.

Six...

Tears roll down my face. My shoulders sag.
Sonia stands a few metres away. Except she's not Sonia.
She's my mum.

She's crying too, because we both know she can't stay.
She wants to hug me like when I was little. But she can't.

Five...

Jo's in her usual storytelling position. She's mid-sentence, animated as ever. I'm watching her, smiling with anticipation as she tells us about something silly or impossible. Derek insists he's heard the story before, but even he looks entertained.

We all burst out laughing, throwing our heads back.

We're happy.

Four...

I'm eating lunch outside the library when Ms. Donnington walks past and waves. She doesn't make a fuss when I'm with my friends. She's always known what I need without asking.

I miss our sessions.

But maybe I don't need them anymore.

Three...

"Get in, you lot! We've got a Goalball tournament to get to," says Dad.

"Thanks for picking us up, Sir."

"I've told you before, Jo. Don't call me Sir– call me Patrick."

Jo laughs and starts quizzing Dad on Goalball rules again. He's clueless, but she's patient. And he's trying. That's what matters.

Two...

We drive past the boab tree– now full of leaves.
And there she is.
Mum.
Leaning against it, smiling, waving at me.
Though I feel the sadness, I've learned to accept my new reality.
I wave back.

One...

I release the ball--- s a curved shot to the bottom left corner.
I hear squeaking as the other team scrambles to block it.
But then...
"Out of play!" calls the referee.
I missed.

The other team takes possession. There mustn't be much time left. I hear the jingle of the ball as it's released from the opposing team's hand.

I hear the jingling get louder—it's coming fast. Left side. Jo's side.

She needs to make the block.

I hear her move into position and her groans as she stretches.

Whoosh.

The ball hits the back of the net.

They've scored.

"Quick Jo, grab the ball!" urges Derek.

But it's too late.

The horn sounds.

The game is over.

I lay flat on my back, exhausted.

Disappointed, too— but I push that aside and sit up, pulling off my eye shades.

I see the other team jumping and hugging, smiling wide.

I can't help but smile back.

I walk over and shake each of their hands.

Dad walks straight up and pulls me into a hug. It

surprises me— I'm still getting used to that.

"I'm proud of you, Owen. You played really well," he says.

"Thanks Dad."

"You know who else would've been proud?"

I frown, unsure what he means.

"Your Mum, kiddo. Your Mum would have been so proud of you. Not just for how you played, but for how you handled yourself out there."

I pretend to wipe the sweat away from my forehead but as I do I trail the back of my hand lower so that it also wipes away the few tears that have started to well in my eyes.

"Excuse me. Owen, is it?" comes a man's voice.

I turn. A tall, athletic-looking man stands smiling, his hand outstretched.

I shake it, unsure.

"Um, yeah. I'm Owen."

"Heck of a game you played. I'm Scott, coach of the State Goalball team."

"Hi Scott, I'm Patrick— Owen's Dad."

"Nice to meet you. Look, I'll get straight to the point. Owen, do you have a visual impairment?"

"Yes... I mean... no. I did. But not anymore," I

stammer.

"Ah. Well, I'm really happy for you. That must be incredible. But... it's a loss for us. I would've loved to coach you. You've got real potential. But as you probably know, professional Goalball teams follow strict rules. Every player must have a visual impairment to compete."

"Yeah... I understand."

"Still, thank you, Scott. We appreciate your kind words," says Dad.

Jo approaches with her head down.

"Jo, we were super close. I'm sorry I didn't score that last one," I say.

"But it was my fault. I let in that goal," she replies.

"We all let in goals. It's not your fault," says Derek.

"Yeah, Derek's right. You were amazing, Jo. Besides, in a few weeks, this will be one of your stories," I tease.

"Yeah," Derek laughs. "A classic Jo story."

Jo looks at us both. A small smile begins to spread across her face.

"Yes, well it definitely has the makings of a Jo story, doesn't it?" she says, laughing loudly.

Derek and I roll our eyes.

"Okay you three, are we ready to hit the road?" asks

Dad.

"Wait, Owen– your eye shade. Don't forget to give it back to Coach Cardiff," instructs Derek.

"Nah, it's mine. What? I like to wear it sometimes... reminds me of what it used to be like," I say.

EPILOGUE

SONIA

"Did you get the horse? Mum, come on! Did Grandma and Grandpop buy you a horse for your 10th birthday?" I ask.

"Didn't I finish telling you that story already?" teases Mum.

"No, you didn't! You were up to the bit about when they made you your favourite breakfast, pancakes with maple syrup and ice cream, and then they measured your height against the boab tree they planted the day you were born. And then you were going to tell me how you went out into the stables. Remember?"

"Was I?" Mum gives me her best puzzled expression,

but I can see the slight upturn in the corner of her lips showing she's just messing around.

"Mum, you're smiling. I can see."

"Okay, okay. I'll tell you the rest of that story. But first, there's a very important one I need to tell you. Don't worry, it's short."

"Two stories in one night? Yeah!!"

She laughs. "Yes, you can have two stories in one night."

She settles onto the bed, sitting up next to me, and gives my shoulders a tight squeeze to make sure I'm tucked in. "Okay, so this story involves a man, his son, and a doctor."

"That doesn't sound like a good story."

"Patience, Owen. The boy was in a terrible accident and was left blind. But recently, he had started seeing what looked like a kaleidoscope of colours in his vision. This was huge, because since the accident he'd only ever seen shadows. With each episode, the colours lasted longer than before."

"What accident?" I ask.

"It was a car accident, Owen. A horrible one. Anyway, the dad told his son not to get his hopes up, but that they needed to go to the doctor to find out why he was seeing colours. The boy thought it meant his sight was coming back."

"And? Was it?" I ask, now genuinely intrigued.

"Well, after the boy explained to the doctor what he'd been seeing..."

"... The colours?" I interrupt.

"Yes, the colours. The doctor said it was a very good sign that his eyesight might be returning, but they needed to run some tests to find out what was going on."

"Tests? What kind of tests?"

"They had to put drops in his eyes, use a special machine to look at the back of his eye, and perform a patch test."

"What's a patch test?" I ask, uncertain.

Mum gives me another squeeze in that way that says I ask too many questions during her stories— but she'll answer it anyway because she knows I won't stop asking until she does.

"Nothing scary. Just patches over your eyes. Anyway, that's exactly what happened. The boy had patches on his eyes, and after a while, the doctor said he was going to remove them— but he had to keep his eyes closed until he was told to open them..."

* * *

I could see my mum giving my dad all these little looks over breakfast. I knew something was going on. I just hoped it was the horse I'd always wanted."

"It has to be a horse," I say, excited.

"Finally, after all the dishes were done, Mum and Dad told me to come for a walk out the back. They gave some excuse, like they needed help with something. Then, suddenly, they stopped and turned to me. They said I needed to close my eyes and let them guide me across the yard. I was so excited. It was going to be the best birthday ever!"

At this moment, Mum's eyes show just as much excitement as I imagine the ten-year-old version of her did that day. Her bright green eyes are glistening, a large smile beaming across her face. This is why I love story time with her so much. The way she retells her stories, with the same emotion as when she lived them, makes you feel like you're actually there.

"Well, was it the best birthday ever?" I ask.

"Looking back, yeah, I'd say it was. Mum and Dad stopped walking and told me to stay still and keep my eyes closed. Then they said, 'After the count of three, you can open your eyes.'

One...

Two...

Three...

Open your eyes. Nothing.

Open your eyes. Nothing.

"Open your eyes, Owen," I hear Dad say.

"It's okay, Owen. Whenever you're ready, just open your eyes and describe what you can see," says Dr. Simmons.

I feel like I've been thrust back to the time in the hospital after the accident, too scared to open my eyes in case I see... nothing. What if the colours were just a glitch? A trick?

But I remind myself: I'm better than those thoughts now. Things in my life are actually really good. Don't get me wrong, I want to see again, but it doesn't have to be right now. I'm doing okay. I have friends. I play Goalball. My dad comes to watch.

So, I decide that no matter what happens now, I'll be okay. And with that, I open my eyes.

The shock hits me hard in the face like a force pressing down. It's bright— too bright. I squint and use the back of my hand to shield my eyes. At the same time, I'm desperate to know if I can see. I blink. Once. Twice.

The dark shadows are gone.

Objects begin to appear in front of me... as if by magic.

But it's not magic.

They were there all along.

The only difference is... now I can *see* them.

* * *

"What did you see when you opened your eyes, Mum?" I ask.

"It was beautiful. I'd never seen anything quite like it," she says.

"The horse?" I ask impatiently.

"Sonia," she replies simply.

"Sonia?" I repeat, baffled.

"Yes. My beautiful horse. Sonia."

About the Author

J A Hunter was born and raised in Perth, Western Australia. Through her love of storytelling, she turned a lifelong dream into reality in 2022 when she began writing her debut novel, *Echoes of the Boab.*

Teaching middle school grade students ignited her passion to help young children grapple with real-world issues through the creation of characters who mirror those struggles.

J A Hunter hopes to foster resilience in young readers by exploring relatable problems and offering stories that resonate with their experiences.